John,

NO GOING BACK

Hope you enjoy the third
part of the trilogy

Chris Orr

Very Best

[illegible]

ISBN: 9798728488217

Cover Photo by Dimitry Anikin on Unsplash
Back Cover Photo by
Click and Learn Photography on Unsplash

My dear wife Hilda and four children
Catherine, David, Kerry, and Lisa.

Chapter 1

Ireland 1868

Mary was very busy buying stuff at the Moville fair. The town was packed on this nice spring day with folks who had come in from the hills with horse carts full of fresh country produce. People seemed to have forgotten that it was only ten years since the great famine had ended, and there was a real sense of new beginnings - even laughter - at some of the stalls, as old men told stories of times past. Moville was basically one long street with shops. There was a square in the middle of it with a side road leading to Carndonagh. Mary walked to the top of the hill which led on to Greencastle, and there she came across the last stall selling fresh fish.

'Hello Cahill,' Mary called over to him. 'Your fish are looking good today,' she laughed.

'Aye Mary, it's still hard to convince people to move away from potatoes, but we're getting there.'

'I still think of me da every time I buy fish, Cahill, but it's a long time ago now.' Cahill picked up a small box and placed some fresh fish in it before handing it to Mary.

'I knew your father, Mary, and he wouldn't want you to be living in the past. It's time now to forget and feed your family some good food. This box is on me.'

Mary reluctantly accepted the box and took a deep breath. 'You're a good man, Cahill. I'll repay your kindness.'

'You already have, miss. Your husband, Thomas, gave me money during the famine; otherwise I wouldn't be here.'

Mary walked back down the hill of the main street to find her carriage parked by the harbour. She had just passed the post office when the postman leaving the shop called after her.

'Mrs. Sweeney, there's a telegram from England for Thomas. I was about to deliver it, so if you wouldn't mind taking it for him that would save me a wee trip.'

'No bother at all, Seamus. I'll see that he gets it.'

When Mary arrived home Thomas was working at his old boat down by the pier.

'Telegram from England,' she called 'I'll leave it by the door.'

Thomas closed off the boat's engine, wiped his oily hands on a rag and walked slowly towards the house.

'It's from Richard,' he called through the open door, and then went very quiet. Mary appeared back at the door. 'What's wrong Thomas?'

Thomas re-read the telegram to make sure there was nothing else. 'It just says to come at once. It sounds urgent!' Thomas handed the telegram to Mary. 'Very strange, Mary; very strange indeed.

No word of what the problem might be. There must be something wrong with my estate.'

'We have Michael and Charity's wedding in two weeks so you can't be away too long.'

Thomas was tired of adventures and just wanted a quiet life, since his last trip to America ended so badly. 'I'll ride over to John. He's so good at arranging travel, Mary. I really don't want any more problems right now.'

Mary came and gave him a big hug. 'It'll be OK, Thomas. God will look after everything.'

Thomas turned and looked into Mary's eyes, shaking his head. 'I hope so.'

He went round to the stables and led his favourite mare out, saddled her up, swung onto her back, and galloped off down the driveway towards Moville. He hadn't ridden so fast for many years and now enjoyed the wind blowing in his face. However, his heart was pounding as he thought of what might be wrong in England.

Arriving at John's house, Thomas spotted Martha coming out of the front door with her two children.

'Afternoon Martha! How lovely you all look on this spring day,' he complimented her as he slid off his horse.

'If you're looking for John, he's down by the shore with your Michael, doing some fencing.'

Thomas walked over to say hello to the children. Martha sounded flustered.

'When I proposed to John,' she grumbled, 'I told him I would look after the simple things in life if he would take care of the complicated things. Well, had I known how complicated children were I may have had second thoughts,' Martha moaned, as she put the baby into a pram.

'It gets easier, Martha, as time goes on,' Thomas laughed, as he put his arm around the shoulder of her four year old son. 'Sure it won't be long till this young man will be helping you.'

'John seems more interested in making this estate work than he does in his children,' Martha mumbled.

'I would doubt that, girl. It's just that it has taken all his time to make this huge estate pay its way again after he released all the tenants from paying rent.'

Martha shrugged her shoulders and walked off down the driveway. John walked around the back of the house and headed for the fields down by the shore.

'Well, what are ye two lads up to?' he shouted, as he came up behind them.

John turned around. 'Good afternoon, sir. And to what do we owe this unusual visit?' John asked, smiling, as he tied the last post of the fence to the wall.

'I need your expert travel advice, John. Have to go to England in a hurry.'

Thomas came over and helped Michael tie the last strand of wire he was holding. 'I was wondering where my son was spending his days. Might have known you were helping my old friend.'

'Less of the 'old' Thomas, if you want me to book tickets for you,' John laughed 'But what's the rush to get back to England? I thought Richard had sorted out all the problems that the last manager had caused.'

'It took Richard nearly two years to rescue my estate as that gangster had sold off five hundred acres of my land - which I'll never get back. Officially, as the law stands, the owner's deeds are worthless, but I have no intention of trying to reclaim it.'

'Any idea why Richard needs you now, Thomas?'

'No, but it doesn't sound too good, so if you could get me there as quickly as possible I'd be very grateful.'

'Right then, let's get going. I've had enough of fencing for one day.'

As they all turned and headed back to the house, Thomas turned to his son, Michael, and enquired quietly. 'Everything going well for the wedding plans, son?'

Michael dropped his head and looked at the ground as he walked along. 'Not sure, Da. Some days I worry about Charity. She doesn't seem as happy as she was a few years ago. Maybe it's just nerves, but I just can't seem to get answers from her.'

Thomas was quiet for a while and as they reached the yard entrance, he said, 'Make sure you're doing the right thing, son. The person you marry must be the best friend in the world and someone you could never be without.'

Michael was about to answer when John returned. Thomas put his arm around his son's shoulders and they walked the last fifty yards without talking.

Thomas mounted his horse and was about to ride home when he turned to Michael. 'Do you know where your sister is?'

'She's still not back from work yet, Da. Last night she caught the last coach from Derry, which gets into Moville at eight.'

Thomas rode on.

Colleen finished work at five and decided she would go into the city centre to see the big, new, fancy building, Austin's Department Store. She walked up Shipquay Street towards The Diamond. It was full of people leaving work to browse in all the different shops. Even though her father was wealthy and she had no need to work, she had decided that once she turned eighteen she would get her own job. She had tried a number of places, but with little formal education it was hard to find work. However, eventually, she found an office job with the Lough Swilly Railway Company. They were the first company to start a railway line from Derry to Donegal, and they had big plans to expand their network all over the North West. The job was boring, but she managed to still have fun with some of the other workers, who enjoyed her refreshing sense of humour.

As she went to cross the road a horse and carriage came from the top of the street at full speed. The horse had bolted, and the driver was trying to stop it. Suddenly she was grabbed from behind and pushed to the ground. She looked up in shock and realised that she was within seconds of being run over by the coach. A young man was standing over her and reached out his hand to lift her up. 'Are you alright, ma'am?' he asked, staring down at her with dark brown eyes.

Mary could hardly speak but managed to brush the dust off her dress. 'I don't know how to thank you, sir,' she stammered. 'I didn't hear the carriage as I was away in a daydream. The horse would have killed me if you hadn't grabbed me.'

'You are too young and pretty to die yet,' the young man laughed and walked on to cross the road.

Colleen had never seen such a handsome man in her life - and his smile was so genuine. 'Excuse me sir, you can't just walk away,' she called after him. 'I mean ... I owe my life to you. I'd like to thank you, somehow.'

'Well maybe we will meet again some day - if it's meant to be. He went to walk away, then paused. 'What might your name be, if I may ask?'

'Colleen, sir,'

He touched his hat and walked on up the street.

Colleen walked slowly back down the street deep in thought. Her life had just been saved by the most handsome man she had ever seen. He seemed so nice - yet there was something mysterious about him. She felt shocked and yet entranced at the same time as she made her way to the six o'clock coach to Moville.

The coach was packed, so the company had put on a second one. She climbed in and found she was sitting opposite a well-dressed business man who was reading a newspaper. As they approached Culmore the man put down his paper and noticed the girl sitting opposite him for the first time.

'Where are you travelling to, miss?' he asked suddenly, taking Colleen by surprise, as she gazed at a heavily laden ship sailing up the River Foyle.

'Moville, sir.' She felt a bit uncomfortable.

'Very good. I'm going to Greencastle. It's a lovely evening.'

Colleen just smiled and turned back to look at the river.

'Do you work in the city, young lady?' The man continued.

'I do, sir. I work for the Londonderry and Lough Swilly Railway Company as a clerk.'

'That sounds like a dull job for such a bright young lady.'

'I get by, sir, and it gives me something to do.' Colleen was nervous, as they were the only people in the coach.

'You look very like a lady I know from Greencastle. You wouldn't be related to Mary Sweeney, would you, by any chance?'

'She's my ma.'

'I thought so,' the man laughed. 'I do all the legal work for your parents. In fact I'll be meeting with them next week.'

Colleen relaxed a little. 'May I ask you your name, sir?'

'William McFarland, my dear, but most people just call me Billy,'

The coach stopped at Muff and a woman with a child got on. Colleen was glad that the conversation was over and the crying child became a welcome distraction.

An hour later the coach pulled up in Moville Main Street and Colleen went to step down when the man touched her arm and said. 'I'm looking for a bright young girl for my office. If you're interested ask your father to contact me and we could talk terms.'

Colleen pulled away and just muttered, 'Thank you,' as she stepped down.

Michael was waiting for her with their own coach and soon they were racing home.

Chapter 2

Thomas was the only person to step off the train at the country station. He walked towards the gate when a guard stepped out of the office and blew his whistle to let the train leave. 'Very quiet tonight, sir. Are you lost?'

'No, thank you.' Thomas replied, changing his suitcase to his other arm. 'Just waiting for a friend.'

Just then Richard appeared, seeming flustered and out of breath.

'Well, my friend, how are you?' asked Thomas, as he gave Richard a hug.

'Could be better, Thomas. Will tell you all on the way home.'

They climbed into the luxury coach and Thomas lay back on the seat, tired of travelling.

'I'm sorry for bringing you here in such a panic Thomas. It's just that something has arisen that only you can sort out.'

Thomas smiled. 'Did our dam bust, Richard'?

'No it did not, Thomas,' Richard scolded. 'We were too clever for that to have happened.'

'Well then, what on earth is this great panic?' Thomas yawned.

'We were going to bed late one night when we heard a faint knocking on the front door. When I opened the door a young woman dressed in very dirty clothes with wet hair hanging down over her face was kneeling by the door. When I went to speak to her she collapsed. Ann helped me bring her into the house where we got her dried off and gave her some food. She told us that she had walked from Manchester and had been on the road for a long time. She then told us her story - which I will now shorten.

Apparently Lord Shrewsbury employed a French nanny called Renee to look after Edward and Christina forty five years ago. Unknown to anyone, including his wife, he had an affair with her, and she became pregnant. To avoid scandal he sent her away with a very large sum of cash, and she ended up living in Manchester where she had her baby, Simone. Simone was brought up very well, but their money started to run out two years ago and, eventually, they fell on hard times. Renee died six months ago so Simone had to try and fend for herself. Her mother told her who her real father was, and that he lived near Shrewsbury, so for the last two months she has been searching for him till, eventually, she made her way to our front door.'

Thomas was dumbfounded. He answered slowly. 'So then...if she's the daughter of Lord Shrewsbury - and she may not be - then she would be the only surviving blood relative!'

Richard nearly choked. 'Gosh, I never thought of that, Thomas. Would she then have any claim on our estate?'

The coach arrived at the front door of the house but the two of them didn't move.

'She would have no claim legally, Richard, as Sir Henry's will was very clear that the estate is mine. However she may have a moral right to something.'

'Thomas, you are getting too soft, lad. The girl could be a complete fraud - and how are we to know?'

Thomas got out of his seat and went to climb down out of the coach. 'There are always means of finding out the truth, Richard, but why the urgency in disrupting my springtime in Ireland when I'm sure you could have sorted this out my friend?'

Richard jumped out of the coach and grabbed Thomas by the arm.

'You are in for the biggest shock of your life, Thomas. I suggest that when we go in that you help yourself to a very strong drink before meeting the girl.'

'Why would I do that, Richard? Does she have a weapon?'

Richard pulled Thomas around to face him.

'Thomas,' he paused 'She is identical to your Christina. So much so that if I had not seen Christina die I would have thought it was she who came to our door! Not only does she look like her, she also has the same character. It's very scary, and I don't know how I am going to introduce you to her.'

Thomas started walking to the door. 'Come, come my friend. It can't be that bad. I don't drink any more so you'll have to make me a strong cup of tea,' he laughed.

Richard asked the valet to bring Thomas's case in, and then followed him into the hallway. Thomas stopped and took a deep breath as all his memories came flooding back of the happy days he had spent with Christina. Richard was very agitated, suggesting that they go right towards the dining room and have some tea.

'I see you're spending plenty of my money redecorating the place.' Thomas sank down on a new soft chair.

'If you had seen the house when we returned two years ago, it was downright criminal what the estate manager had done! The place had been derelict for a year as he had fled leaving doors and windows open so that much of the house was ruined with damp. He let his dogs sleep on all the furniture and his children had carved their names on some of our antique tables. It's only in the last month that I can say it's restored to what it was in your time.'

Thomas sighed. 'So when am I going to meet this woman?'

Just then Ann came in with a butler bearing two cups of tea.

'Great to see you, Ann - and looking wonderful as usual,' Thomas said as he stood up and gave her a hug. 'Thank you both for taking on this huge task. I should have come back from Ireland to help you.'

'Has Richard introduced you to Simone yet, Thomas?' Ann asked cautiously.

'That's her name, then? I believe it's going to happen after I drink my tea, Ann.'

'You'll need more than tea, Richard. I'm not jesting.' She looked serious.

'Now you two are getting me worried.' Thomas poured himself some tea and stared out the window at the fountains that Christina had designed. The butler came back into the room. 'Pardon me, sir, but the young lady is now in the drawing room, as you requested.'

'Thank you, Andrew. We'll come now.' Richard moved to the door.

'Not we, Richard. I must go and meet her on my own.' Thomas moved quickly to the door.

Richard and Ann tried to stop him, but he was up and out the door before they could even speak.

Thomas went straight to the drawing room and opened the door with a heavy shove.

Upon entering, he suddenly stood transfixed. The blood drained from his face. Christina was standing in front of him - only it wasn't Christina - it was a woman called Simone!

'You must be Thomas.' Simone spoke softly, looking intensely at Thomas. Thomas struggled to catch his breath. 'I'm sorry. It's just...it's just that you are like an identical twin to my late wife, Christina, who died twenty three years ago.' He murmured sadly. ' You are so alike it's as if she has come back from the grave. I'm really sorry for scaring you.'

'I was born forty five years ago, so my mother would have known Christina very well.'

'Yes I suppose she would, but that was even before I came here and met Christina.'

Simone motioned for Thomas to sit down with her on the couch. 'I'm very sorry that your wife died, sir. I'm told she was a very lovely person.'

'You even speak like her.' Thomas had tears in his eyes. 'You are the same height, the same build, and the same long blonde hair and yet you are born from a French mother. It's so very strange.'

'My mother was very pretty too, sir, and that was her downfall with Lord Shrewsbury. My mother loved him, as he did her, but he realised if anyone found out then he would lose everything. She told me before she died that he was exceptionally good to her and gave her a very large sum of money that would have lasted a lifetime if my mother had not wasted it on a lavish lifestyle'

Thomas turned and looked at her with real compassion. 'You have had a sad life then, Simone; first to have no father, and then to lose your mother so young. It's all so tragic'

'No, sir. I had a very happy life until my mother died. She told me who my real father was in her last few days and said I should try and find his family'.

'I think I need to take time to process all this, Simone.' Thomas stood up and walked to the window, shaking inside.

'I loved my Christina like she was the only person in the world. When she died it took me years to get over her death. I eventually married Mary, in Ireland, whom I love dearly. Yet I still could never forget Christina. I just can't believe that you are not her. Even your blue eyes and smile. Are you sure you are the daughter of a French lady'? he asked, shaking his head.

'I would hardly think Lord Shrewsbury would have sent my mother away if she was not carrying me.' Simone got up and stood beside him.

'Forgive me,' he said, as he was conscious that he was staring right into her face.

'There's nothing to forgive, Thomas. Your friend Richard showed me pictures of your late wife and I was deeply shocked. I thought I was looking at a picture of myself.'

Just then Richard and Ann came in, looking distressed.

'I hope you both are quite all right,' stammered Richard. 'Perhaps you would like a glass of brandy.'

Thomas relaxed and smiled 'We're both fine, thank you, Richard. It will just take me some time to adjust to the shock. I thought Christina had come back from the dead, and you were quite right to warn me.'

'I think perhaps we should all take a walk before dinner.' Ann suggested as she took Simone by the arm.

'Good idea, Ann. I'll show Thomas the improvements to the gardens.'

Ann took Simone out the front door while Thomas and Richard walked through the house to the back garden.

'Well?' enquired Richard

'You were right, my friend. This is unbelievable! I just don't know what to do. It's like my old life has been slapped in my face, and just when I was getting settled with life in Donegal.'

'What are you going to do, Thomas?'

Thomas sighed deeply and looked at the new apple trees that Richard had planted.

'I wanted to take her in my arms and kiss her...to remind her of all the fun we used to have riding around the estate... tell her what has happened since we last met ...tell her how I missed her, and how my life had ended when she left.'

'I was afraid you would say that. This is not good.' Richard was shaking his head up and down.' You did that once before, which started a whole new life for both of us. You have too much to lose this time, Thomas.'

Thomas laughed. 'Don't worry. I will not be kissing her. I have a wife and family who I love deeply back home and I will never chance losing them again.'

'What are we going to do with her then? We can't just send her on her way. After all, this was her father's home.'

'Don't say a word yet. We have to find out if she really is Lord Shrewsbury's daughter. She certainly looks like it and, if she is, she might even be entitled to be called Lady Shrewsbury.' Thomas turned and looked at Richard who looked aghast. Thomas laughed. 'Your face is a picture, Richard. It's all right, my friend. You will not lose your home and money - that is until I throw you out,' he joked.

'Will we keep her in the house.? It would be very awkward,' Richard stammered.

'I think the cottage that we both stayed in when we first arrived here would be a good place for her. It's big enough for a family and only half a mile from your house. She would be on her own but close enough to you for company.'

'It would take a month to renovate it but that's a good idea, Thomas.' Richard walked towards the orchard. 'Let me show you all the different fruit trees that I've planted.'

Dinner that evening was more relaxed as Ann had found a new friend in Simone, and Thomas was beginning to find peace. When the main course was complete, Thomas turned to Simone and said kindly, 'Simone.' He paused. 'Please tell us all about your life, from the earliest that you remember. I'm sure your story would be fascinating.'

Chapter 3

It was Sunday, and Mary had just come back from church to make lunch. It was unusually warm for April in Donegal, and she loved the sound of the small waves lapping against the harbour at the front of their house. Colleen strolled out of the front door just as she arrived.

'You're late up, Colleen. I missed you at church today,' Mary said, taking her cardigan off.

'Late night, Ma. Bit tired.' Colleen smiled.

'Late night doing what, miss?' Mary scolded teasingly.

'The girls and meself walked into Moville and back to see if there were any boys about but they must have all been hiding.'

'Hmm...I see. And why would my nineteen year old daughter be looking for boys, now?

'Just for fun, Ma. This place is so quiet. Nothing here to admire but sheep and cows.'

'I was chatting to Billy, our lawyer, this week. He said he was talking to you on the coach one night.'

'Yes. I found him a bit forward. He was asking me a lot of questions.'

'He's not forward, Colleen. He's very well respected here, along with his wife and family. He told me he offered you a job.'

'I didn't know if he was serious or not. Anyway, I have a job, Ma.'

'Yes but working in a legal office in the city would be a very big step up Colleen and not a position that would come up very often.'

'I'll think about it. It means I'd be working in the city centre. That would be nice, I suppose.'

Just then Charity came walking up the lane.

'I see you are up bright and early on this beautiful day. Charity - not like Colleen and Michael,' Mary laughed.

'I like to walk and pray, Mary, especially on Sundays.' Charity gave a big smile as she joined them. 'How are you, Colleen? I love your dress.'

'Thanks, Charity. I'm doing well. Just pondering over a few things right now, so I'm sorry I haven't had a chance to talk with you this week.'

'Charity has been helping me with housework,' Mary started, as she took out a tablecloth to cover the wooden table. 'I think it's time she made an adventure to find a better job - maybe in the city with you Colleen.'

'Would you like that Charity?' Colleen asked, sitting down at the table.

'Not quite sure what I would like to do. All I did with my daddy was clean the house. He did want me to do something useful with my life. That's what he said before he died, anyway.'

'It doesn't seem like it's coming six years since we were all in America,' Colleen sighed 'Those were very strange days.'

Michael suddenly appeared at the door with his shirt half on and his hair uncombed.

Nice of you to join us for spring, my son,' Mary scolded. 'I think, since you are up last, you should make lunch for us all.'

Michael went over and hugged Charity and they sat down opposite Colleen.

'Right so,' Mary sighed 'It's as well I had a big pot of chicken soup made for lunch. Colleen, give me a hand to bring it out. There's no point eating inside in this heat.'

'Da had better be back for our wedding, Charity.' Michael snuggled up to her. 'After all, he did say he would give you away.'

Charity didn't respond but looked anxiously down, and her hands that were clasped.

'Are you all right, my love?' Michael asked, as he took her hands in his own.

'Yes Michael, but can we go for a walk after lunch?'

'Sure we can. I would like to show you the boat John and I have been building quietly, as long as you say nothing.'

Mary came out the door with the soup, followed by Colleen holding plates and spoons.

Thomas arrived down to the breakfast room where Richard, Ann, and Simone had already started eating.

'It's not like you to sleep in, Thomas,' Richard laughed.

'This house is far too comfortable. Why on earth did I agree to let you live here?' Thomas replied filling his plate with scrambled eggs.

'Because no one else would take on the responsibility of an ageing estate that was losing money and turn it round to make you a fortune.'

'Yes but look at the lifestyle I am providing for you. I suppose the locals think you are the new Lord Shrewsbury.'

'Yes. It got me thinking a title would go rather well for Ann and I, as well as our entire family,' he laughed.

'Talking about family, Richard, where are your children?'

'They had breakfast early. Nanny has taken them to the new play area in the garden.'

'I was very moved by your life story last night. Simone. Your Mother must have been a very special woman.'

'She was, sir. Her name was Renee. She was from Paris and had worked for many rich people before coming to England. She was highly thought of, but her downfall was that she was very pretty.'

'It is quite extraordinary that you look so much like Christina. Christina was very like her mother. It's extraordinary how much you resemble her,' Thomas mused.

'I'm sad that I only got to meet my father a few times when I was young. I believe he was a very kind man too.' Simone smiled at Thomas.

'He was an exceptional man, Simone. He didn't behave like most of the aristocracy. He left this life far too early. The tragedy was that didn't even get to see how happy his daughter had become in her last few days.'

Richard joined in, finishing his tea. 'I'm quite sure that Lord Shrewsbury would never have thought that his entire estate and fortune would end up in the hands of a poor young Irish boy either.'

'You are from Ireland?' Simone asked, surprised.

'Yes. I am from a place called Donegal, which is where I now live with my wife and two children.

'Thomas is very wealthy but he has a very kind heart, Simone. He prefers to give everything away,' Ann interjected.

'Only because I had nothing to start with, Ann,' Thomas answered standing up and moving to the window. 'If you start your life with nothing it's good to remember that when you leave this life you will have nothing either, so what you have in between really doesn't matter that much.'

Richard changed the subject. 'I was thinking, folks, that it being such a nice sunny day, maybe we could take a drive to the lake so Thomas can see how his crazy idea turned out.'

Thomas turned from the window 'Great idea, Richard, but first Simone and I must take a walk.'

He went around the far side of the breakfast table and held out his hand to Simone. She looked embarrassed and glanced over at Ann for approval.

'We we'll be ready for your coach ride in an hour,' Thomas shouted back as they left the room.

'These are the most beautiful fountains I have ever seen, sir.' Simone stopped, and shook her head.

'Christina designed these. By the way, no need to call me 'sir'. 'Thomas' will quite suffice,' he laughed.

'She must have been a very clever person, Thomas,' Simone said softly.

'She was quite the most amazing human being that God ever placed on this earth.' Thomas sat down by the moving fountain and motioned for Simone to join him. 'This is where we first kissed and also where, a year later, she tried to tell me that she knew she was going to die. To be perfectly honest, it's just so strange now being here with someone who looks so much like her. It is like eighteen years have not passed.'

Simone put her hand in the pool and let the water run through her hands. Thomas stood up as if to shake himself out of a dream. 'Christina used to do that too.' His eyes were watering and he tried to clear his voice.

Suddenly he steadied himself. 'I must be very straight with you, Simone, so that you understand fully where you stand right now. Legally we have to go through a process to verify that you are the daughter of Lord Shrewsbury. I believe you that you are his daughter, without question, but the law will not be convinced by looks. If it can be proved that, indeed, you are his daughter, then we shall have to sort out all the legalities. In fact we will need to know if you are entitled to be called 'Lady Shrewsbury'. I personally believe you will.' Thomas smiled and sat down again. 'I must tell you that Christina was left the entire estate when her father died. When she died a year later in childbirth everything came to me. I wanted to return to Ireland to live so I gave the estate to Lord Shrewsbury's brother, Sir Henry, with a guarantee of a life long incomes for Richard as manager and myself. When Sir Henry found out he was dying he signed the entire estate back to me as he had no family of his own.'

Simone stood up and faced Thomas. 'I came here to find out about my father, not his money, and I have no interest in becoming Lady Shrewsbury. I will return to Manchester and try and find work knowing I have found out who I am and have made new friends.'

Thomas stood up again and took Simone by the hand, looking thoughtful. 'There is a very nice cottage on these grounds about half a mile down our driveway. It is where Richard and I lived when we first came to work here. If you are his daughter then we would be quite happy for you to live there on the estate. As Lord Shrewsbury was so good to me then I feel it only right that I should look after you.'

'I will make sure that you have a good income from the estate and Richard and Ann will be nearby to take care of you.'

Thomas took Simone's arm and they walked up to the waiting coach. The trip to the lake was a very quiet affair that day as they all had a lot to think about.'

The next day Thomas announced he was leaving as he had to be back for his son's wedding.

'What do I do with Simone?' Richard asked in panic as walked down the corridor with Thomas.

'Keep her in the house till you get the cottage renovated. I have told her that the cottage will then be hers, once we have legal confirmation that she is Lord Shrewsbury's daughter. I will then give her an income from the estate for life and hopefully she will give us no more bother.'

'What If it turns out that she's not his daughter. Do I just send her on her way?'

'Now Richard, I do not believe you have it in you to be so mean. I'm sure you will find some way of looking after her, if only to give her a job as one of your staff'. Anyhow, I'll leave the problem in your very capable hands.'

Thomas laughed as he ran down the stairs. 'See you shortly, my old friend.'

Michael helped Charity out of her seat when lunch was over. 'Right, girl you want to walk. Come with me now.'

They walked down the lane holding hands. 'It's nearly two miles to John's house. Do you want to walk or shall I get the horses?'

'Walking is fine in this hot weather, Michael.' Charity smiled. 'I'm still scared of those creatures. They just seem to have a mind of their own.'

'The trick is to make them think that, but in reality you control them. It takes a while but in a month they will be doing exactly what you want then to do.' Michael picked up a stick and threw it over the hedge. 'You were very quiet at lunch today, my love. Is there something wrong?'

Charity walked on with her head down before she stopped and looked at Michael. Her eyes were turning moist.

'Michael, I need to talk to you.' She started.

'Well that's what your doing right now,' Michael laughed.

'No. It's serious.' She looked very sad.

Michael picked up another stick and seemed to find the conversation amusing.

'I love you deeply, Michael,' Charity started slowly. 'I deeply appreciate your family rescuing me in America and bringing me here for a new life. I would have been poor all my life, and maybe even dead, if your family had you not been there for me. I was getting on fine till six months ago when Colleen took me to Derry. I found a book in a shop with pictures of the country my father was born and raised in. I suddenly had this strange feeling come over me that I don't belong here.'

'You are scaring me,' Michael said as he stood in front of her.

'People are so nice to me here in Donegal and Derry. They are so polite and kind, but everyone stares at me because I'm the only black person in this part of the country. I know when they pass me in the street they are talking about me. In America there were lots of black people, and white people didn't stare at me like they do here.'

'You're just being over sensitive, Charity,' replied Michael, trying to make her laugh. 'They are only staring at you because you are incredibly pretty, not because you're black.'

'I'm not stupid, Michael. I know what people are thinking.'

'It will take folks a bit of time to get used to seeing someone different, but after a while I'm sure more black people will come here, and soon they will hardly notice.'

'My father talked about life back in Ghana, and both my parents always wanted to go home. They were captured by the English and then sold to men in America. They told me that in their own country they had a poor life, but it was happy. They also had family that they knew they would never see again. All my life they talked about their life back home.' Charity paused and stared at Michael. 'I want to go home and see if I can find any of my family. If I can't find any of them, then I will come back immediately and marry you.'

'And if you find family you will stay?' Michael answered, angrily.

Charity looked down again and shook her head. 'It's something I have to do, Michael, or I will never find peace.' She started to sob. 'I want to marry you, Michael. It's just not the right time.'

There was silence. Then Michael shouted, 'Well it's a bit late now, girl! We're supposed to be getting married next week! What am I supposed to do? Wait here while you sail off to Africa for a few years? You want to come back in a few years time expecting me to be waiting for you? Is that right, Charity?'

'I love you Michael - very much. I just find it hard to fit in here when my heart is where my roots are.'

Michael turned and started walking back to this house. 'Well, you tell that to my family,' he shouted back. Charity sat down on a large stone and sobbed and sobbed.

Chapter 4

John was waiting for Thomas at the end of the driveway as his coach pulled in from Derry.

'Hello Thomas. Did you have a good trip, sir?' John asked, shaking hands with him.

'Every time I leave Ireland, John, something strange happens. As I sat on the ship last night thinking, I decided I will never go away again. This is home and this is where I am staying.'

John laughed 'So what adventure did you get up to this time?'

'You simply would not believe it, my friend. I'll tell you sometime.'

They started walking towards the house when John quietly broke the silence. 'Listen Thomas. It's none of my business, but I thought I should pre-warn you of some bad news waiting for you.'

Thomas stopped and turned to John. 'Who's dead?' he asked, anxiously.

'Oh goodness no! No one has died. It's just something concerning Charity which I'll leave the family to tell you. I just wanted you, as a friend, to be aware of some bad news.'

'Don't tell me she's pregnant.'

'Oh no, no, sir! No scandal involved, and I have told you enough already.'

Thomas sighed and quickened his pace towards the house. 'Did you get a chance to find out about my business in Derry. Any news about the fire?'

'I did, and again it's something I would like to talk with you about over a drink or a meal; maybe not just not right now.'

Thomas turned and slapped John on the back 'I couldn't have a more loyal friend in the whole world. I hope you and Martha are doing well.'

'We are, thank you, but I think Martha is finding it challenging bringing up two children.'

'Only two, John? What's keeping you?' Thomas laughed, as he quickened his pace.

Mary was hanging washing out on the line when she saw Thomas coming up the driveway. She dropped the clothes and ran to meet him, giving him a big hug. He picked her up and gave a twirl.

'I'm so pleased to see you, my love. A week seemed a very long time,' Mary gasped.

'It has been a lifetime, Mary, but I'll tell you all about that later. John tells me you have some bad news for me.' Mary took Thomas by the arm and sat him down by the wooden picnic table.

'The wedding is off,' she announced sadly.

Thomas shook his head in disbelief. 'What! Why?'

'Charity isn't happy here and wants to go to Africa to find any living family. She says that she finds it hard to be herself here being the only black person.'

Thomas sat and looked at the table for a long time before he spoke. 'Where is she now?'

'Ever since she talked to Michael, she has been in her room. She won't come down, and I've been bringing food up to her every day.'

'How long till dinner'?

'About an hour. Why?

Thomas got up and walked towards the house. 'Leave this to me, but make sure a place is set for Charity.'

Thomas knocked on Charity's door.

'Come in, Mary,' answered Charity with a very sad voice.

'Hello Charity,' Thomas smiled as he entered her room. 'I hope you don't mind if I step into your room for a minute.'

'Thomas!' Charity exclaimed. 'I thought you were in England!'

'I was indeed but I rushed home for a wedding that I hear is not happening now.'

Charity started to cry and Thomas sat down beside her, putting his arm around her. She sobbed for a while. Then Thomas pulled up a chair and sat opposite her.

'Listen carefully to me, Charity. I am not cross with you. I think you're doing the right thing.'

Charity stopped crying and looked up in surprise.

'When I first went to England in 1842, I was eighteen, and from a very poor background. My mother couldn't even afford her own house but she was taken in by Mary's mother. A stranger showed me immense kindness and he ended up getting me a great job. After three years I was assigned a big project on a huge English estate. It was there I fell in love with a beautiful English girl who was the daughter of the estate owner. We got married and suddenly I became very wealthy. When she and her father died in the same year I was left in a huge house with just my work friend Richard. I was very sad for a long time. If I had stayed in England, no doubt I would have got over it and maybe remarried eventually. However, one day I decided that I would go home and start afresh in Ireland. I left Richard to run my estate, and came home to my own people. When I got home, I fell in love again with my childhood friend, Mary, and we married. So you see, Charity, I totally understand why you want to go back to Africa. When you get there you might find all sorts of people you can enjoy your lost culture with. On the other hand you may not find anyone, or not even like the country at all.

Either way, you will have done the courageous thing - that is to try.'

Charity looked up at Thomas and smiled.

'No matter how hard it is, please write to tell us how you are getting on,' Thomas said, as he stood up. Charity hugged Thomas. 'Thank you so much. You are such a kind man.'

'I wanted to look after your father as well as you. It was so cruel what those men did to him.'

'He thought you were the kindest man he had ever met. He had the greatest respect for you.'

Thomas stood up and moved to the door. 'Now young lady come down for dinner in an hour. We have a lot of planning to do for your trip.'

Thomas talked to the family before Charity came down for dinner. The only person who didn't speak all evening was Michael. Thomas made a short speech at the table about Charity and wished her well on her travels, but Michael got up and walked out the back door. Thomas waited a few seconds, then followed him.

'I know this is very hard for you, Michael,' Thomas called, as he followed Michael into the stables.

Michael carried on getting a saddle for his horse, ignoring his father.

'Where are you going at this time of the evening, Michael?' he asked him gently.

'To meet my friends in Moville, Da. That's if they haven't all run off to another country as well.'

'I know you love her deeply but you have to let her go, Son.' Thomas came round and blocked him taking the horse out of the stable.

'Why did she keep me going for five years, Da, when she all she wanted to do was to go home?'

'It only came to her six months ago, Son, and we must respect that.'

'Everyone likes her here, Da. She has no need to run away.' Michael stroked the horse's head.

'Yes, Son, but can you imagine living in Africa and being the only white person? No matter how kind people would be to you they would still look at you as being very different and you would probably feel the same way as Charity.'

'Can I go now, Da?' Michael asked, still annoyed.

Thomas moved out of his way. 'Be careful on the roads, Son. It'll be getting dark in a few hours.'

Colleen entered the lawyer's office in Clarendon Street in Derry. She walked right up to a lady at the front desk. 'I would like to speak to William McFarland please,' she said, in her most polite accent.

'Do you have an appointment Miss?' the lady answered sharply.

'No, but he knows my family and he offered me a job.' Colleen was very nervous.

'Well Miss, it's nearly our closing time and William is just finishing with his last client. I would suggest that you leave me your details and I'll inform him later.'

Just then a door opened and William appeared shaking hands with a gentleman and showing him to the door.

'Ah ha. You came.' He turned when he saw Colleen about to leave. 'I didn't think I would see you again. Please come into my office for a moment.'

William turned to his secretary and asked her to close the office and go on home. That made Colleen even more nervous.

'I'm sorry for calling so late, sir. It's just that I finished work at five and walked from Pennyburn into the town.' Colleen stood nervously in the most grand office she had ever seen.

'Please take a seat, Miss. Forgive me. I've forgotten your name,' William said, as he sat down opposite her at his desk.

'Colleen, sir.'

'Right, Colleen. Let me get straight to the point. For some time now I have been looking for a young person to join my team. I need someone who I can train to be a legal assistant. Your duties would be to learn everything about every client we handle and to assist me when cases go to court. After a few years, if you are good at your job, I would then get you trained as a lawyer, and you could then join our practice. That's a long way away yet, but that would be my goal. I need someone who is presentable, clever and willing to work hard. I will pay more than double of what I presume you are earning now and there'll be plenty of time to relax in your nice house by the sea.'

Colleen sat speechless, staring in disbelief at what he just said.

'Good. That's settled then.' William stood up and moved to open the office door. 'I presume you need to give your employer a week's notice, so I'll give you a start on Monday week.'

Colleen stood up and moved to the door, still barely able to speak. 'Thank you, sir,' she muttered, as she left the building very quickly.

As she walked along The Strand Road towards her coach for home she was in a complete daze. All of a sudden she bumped into a young gentleman who was walking towards her. 'My apologies, sir,' she stammered. 'I wasn't looking where I was going.'

'At least you weren't trying to kill yourself this time in front of a horse,' the gentleman laughed, as he tipped his hat to her.

Colleen looked up in shock and saw it was the same handsome man with the dark brown eyes who saved her life from the bolting horse and coach. 'Oh my goodness, sir, I am so embarrassed.'

'I told you we might meet again if it was meant to be.'

'Ah yes,' she said, flustered. Pardon me, but I must run to catch my coach.'

'I shall keep walking these streets of this city in hope of bumping into you again,' he said. 'Good evening.' He touched his hat again and walked away. Colleen wanted to stay and find out more about him but realised she had only five minutes to get her coach. She smiled all the way home.

The next day John decided to ride over to Thomas's house to talk about business. As he approached the house, Thomas was fixing part of the garden fence. 'I thought you my be employing a man to do that sort of work,' he laughed...'Or a good woman. John, is your Martha free?'

'No sir, she's busy cutting logs around the back for the winter.'

'But it's the middle of the spring, John, and that's very hard labour for a woman!' Thomas drove the last nail into the timber.

'I know, but when we married she said she wanted to do the simple things in life, so if it keeps her happy then I am fine with that.'

'What brings my friend here today, anyway?'

John was about to answer when a horse came up behind them. The black horse was huge and was ridden by a policeman.

Thomas was astonished! 'Lieutenant O'Hare! Is that really you?'

'It is indeed, young Thomas, only I'm not lieutenant any more; just plain old Sergeant Alfred O'Hare at your service,' he said, tipping his hat.

He dismounted from the horse and came over, shaking hands with them both.

'What are you doing here - and in a police uniform?' Thomas asked with amazement.

'Long story, Thomas, but when I left you five years ago, I went home to Cork. I soon discovered that all my few relations had died in the famine. I took over the old homestead and did it up until I ran short on my savings. One day I saw a notice looking for new police recruits in the RIC so I signed up. When they found out I had been a lieutenant in the New York Police Force they made me a sergeant. I was doing fine till a new chief came along. We had disagreements on policies, shall we say, so he had me posted as far away from Cork as is possible. I was sent here to Moville, so I guess at the age of fifty five I will see out my days here.'

'Well, stone the crows, Alfred! That's some story! It'll be good to have a friend in the police. You never know these days what might happen.'

'Actually, Thomas, I came over to let you know about a situation and so that, hopefully, there will never be the need for an official visit.'

Thomas looked alarmed. 'Oh! What is that, Alfred'?.

'Would you happen to know where your son, Michael, might be?'

'In his bed at this time of the day, Alfred,' Thomas answered, suspiciously. 'Why do you ask?.'

'Would you mind checking the house?'

Thomas looked at John before walking towards the front door.

'I'm John Campbell,' John said, smiling at Alfred.

'I know who you are, John. I would never forget a man who came all the way from Ireland to rescue

Mary. It's very nice to see you again.'

'I look after the estate in Moville, sir, and got married to Mary's sister, Martha.'

'Good man. I'll look forward to calling by for a chat one day.'

Thomas and Mary appeared from the house together.

'Lieutenant O'Hare how good to see you again,' Mary said, as she walked over to shake his hand.

'You keep popping up here, and now Thomas tells me you are the new sergeant.'

'I am so, Mary, and it's my honour to meet you again.'

'Michael never came home last night,' Thomas said quietly. 'Were you looking for him?'

Alfred nodded. ' There was a fight in the town last night and a young fella got a bad beating. It seems a group of lads set on him. He didn't get a chance to see who it was but a bystander said he thought your Michael was one of them.'

'What!' exclaimed Thomas. 'Was he sure?'

'Not at this stage, Thomas. It seems the young fella is afraid to press charges, so at this stage I'm going around the possible suspects' parents to warn them how serious this might have been.'

'Quite right, Alfred,' Mary started as she saw how angry Thomas was getting. 'When he comes home he will be dealt with, I can assure you, and he never will be going to Moville again at night.'

Alfred went over to his horse. I hope I can call for tea sometime when I'm passing. It's going to take a while for a new sergeant with an American accent to accepted by the locals.'

'He got some bad news the other day about his wedding plans, so I guess he must have taken it the wrong way.' Thomas said sadly. 'That's not the way to deal with it. I will find him now, Alfred. Thank you again.'

Alfred turned his horse and rode down the driveway. There was silence between the three of them for some time before John spoke. 'I think I know where to find him, folks. Maybe it would be better if I talk to him first.'

Thomas and Mary stood silently looking out to sea before Thomas said, 'you are a good man John. Do what you can.'

John found Michael where he thought he would be. He was sitting alone in a small fish shed on the beach just below the estate. With the door open, he was looking down the River Foyle chewing dulse. John said nothing but came and sat down beside him. They sat for some time before Michael spoke.

'I suppose Da sent you here, John?' he asked, timidly.

'No. When I heard you were missing I knew you would be here,' John answered, kindly.

'I don't know what came over me, John. I have never hit another person in my life.'

'When you are upset Michael it is very hard to predict what a person will do, so it's better to avoid those sorts of situations. The consequences can be very serious.'

'I suppose someone told me da.'

'Not 'someone' Michael - the new police sergeant.'

'Oh no! Is the boy hurt?'

'No. he's fine, but lucky for you he's not pressing charges. Someone who witnessed the fight thought they saw you as one of the attackers, so the sergeant came to warn your da to make sure you are kept out of trouble.'

'I know the boy. He is a nice lad, but he never should have said something about me getting married to a black girl.'

'It'll be a learning time for you, Michael. It's always best to walk away from anyone who insults you - and it's actually more manly.'

'I'll be in big trouble with Da now, John. I don't know how I can go home.'

'They aren't well pleased, Son, but they'll be all right if you let me talk to them first.'

'My ma will probably beat me over me head with her bible,' Michael smiled.

'You deserve that,' John laughed, standing up. 'However, I think you will find you'll be safe enough to venture home. One thing - where's your horse?'

'I have no idea. Probably eating your plants,' Michael joked.

Chapter 5

Thomas was working on his boat 'The Daydream.' It was thirty feet in length and built to withstand a rough sea, with a high bow and a sealed cabin. Although the boat was old, it one of the first local boats to have a steam engine fitted. Thomas wanted that engine so that the boat could take him the short distance from Greencastle to the Atlantic Ocean on a calm day. While he loved the boat, he was still afraid of the sea, having nearly drowned twenty six years ago at the age of eighteen. He would only head out past the mouth of the Foyle when the weather was calm. Today the sea was choppy so he was content to finish painting the boat. Just then John appeared.

'Do you want a hand at painting that old thing or are you just going to stare at it all day?' he laughed as he walked down the pier. Thomas looked up expectantly. He knew John never came for a social visit. He climbed into the boat and joined Thomas by the wheelhouse. 'I was at an interesting meeting in Moville last night,' he mused. Thomas grunted.

'It was with local people who want to see changes in our country.' John cleared his throat. 'They're looking for a new man to stand in the forthcoming parliament elections.'

'Good,' replied Thomas. 'I'll vote for you, for sure.'

'Not me, Thomas. I suggested you,' John said nervously.

Thomas put down his paintbrush and looked at John as if he had taken leave of his senses.

'I'm busy, John. Come back to me when you have something sensible to say,' he said gruffly.

'I'm serious, Thomas. You're always complaining about the way

London treated us during the famine and how you believe it is time for us to govern ourselves. Well, I believe the only way you are going to ever achieve that is if you change the system from the inside.'

'John, I'm forty four. I've had more adventures than most people have had in a lifetime. It's time for me to settle down and enjoy Donegal and a quiet life. Why would I ever want to go and spend my life debating and arguing with people in London?'

'Because everywhere you go you make a difference in people's lives. Just think what you could do for Ireland.'

'I make a difference by causing trouble and by being in the wrong place at the wrong time.'

'If that were true, Thomas, you would have a lot of enemies, but instead you have large numbers of people who want to be your friend.'

'Who want my money, you mean.' Thomas put his paintbrush down and climbed out of the boat. He paused and looked back at John, who seemed very downcast. 'When are the elections?'

John was taken by surprise. He looked up. 'Nominations have to be in by two weeks' time, with the elections in June.' Thomas walked back to the house. John stood looking down at the deck, smiling.

Colleen was very busy looking through reams of legal documents on her desk. She was enjoying her new job but realised that she was being given responsibility way beyond what she thought she was capable of doing. William came in the front door with a briefcase and said, 'Good morning,' to the office secretary, Elaine. Colleen stepped out of her office with a bunch of papers. 'Excuse me, sir. Can you look at these please?'

William turned and followed her into her office and closed the door.

'I think there's a problem here that will affect the court case of one of your clients next week.'

'Well, what might that be, then?' he answered.

'Your client is suing the owner of the building for not revealing that there was a major problem in developing it because of incorrect plans.'

William looked over her shoulder. She moved to one side slightly and continued. 'I have studied the files very carefully and discovered that the plans are indeed incorrect. However, the fault lies with the solicitor who conducted the sale as he failed to notice that part of the building was constructed with a small piece of land that belonged to another person.'

William's face dropped as he looked at the papers. 'This is not good, girl. I was the solicitor who conducted the sale.' He looked at the site map that Colleen had found buried away under a pile of documents. He looked worried as he strode off to his office.

'How did I miss that Colleen? That is so stupid. Right. Leave it to me to sort out. Well done girl. That would have been very embarrassing if it had come up in court,' he called back.

Colleen went back to her desk with a smile on her face.

Michael was helping John paint the last section on the their new boat they had built secretly in John's shed at the back of the estate. 'How are we going to get this into the sea, John? It must be nearly one hundred yards to the water.'

'I wondered about that myself, Michael,' John laughed. 'I might have a plan.'

'Do you think Da will be pleased? It's much better than his old boat and he might take um bridge at me building a better boat.'

'I hope not,' John smiled, as he stood back and looked at the finished boat.

'I thought you and I could go fishing in it, John,' Michael said sadly. My da won't take me.'

'We will, Michael, but it's very important that we keep your Da happy right now as he has a lot on his mind.'

'What's on his mind now, John?' he asked sharply.

'I'll let your da tell you. son. I may have dropped him into another adventure.'

Mary called in to see Rose and Bridget. 'How are the mothers getting on?' she laughed as she entered the front door of their new house. 'Have ye the tea on?'

'If we can find the teapot in this fancy house you put us in,' replied her mother. 'It's like walking a mile to go from one end of the kitchen to the other.'

'Aye, but it's warm, Mother, and it doesn't need a turf fire burning all day.'

Mary waked over to the table and looked inside a large cooking pot. 'What are you cooking, Bridget?

'I made that last night but don't know how to cook it on this fancy range thing that Thomas installed.'

Mary lifted it over to the cooker and placed it on a large ring. 'All you do, Bridget, is open this wee door at the front and with sticks and turf you get a wee fire going. After an hour the whole cooker will be roasting and you just sit and watch the stew cook while you read a book or knit a scarf.'

'We miss the open fire with the crochan for cooking, Mary. It seems dangerous to light a fire inside that thing.'

Mary laughed and started to light the fire for them.

'Now that we live next door I thought I might see more of my son,' Bridget scolded.

'Ah sure I hardly see the man himself. He's always up to something.'

'How did he get on in England?' Rose asked.

'Not sure, Ma. I never asked him as we had the wedding crisis when he got back, and then Michael went missing.'

'Martha told us. Any word from Charity?'

'Nothing yet, Ma. It'll take her months to get to Africa. I wouldn't be surprised if we never hear from her again.'

'She seemed so happy here,' Bridget sighed. 'She was such a nice young lady.'

'She fitted in well with the family, Ma, but just felt awkward when she went to the town or Derry. She said everyone stared at her, so I guess she just wanted to be with her own people.'

'Sad though. She would have made a great wife for my grandson,' Rose sighed.

'Michael was very upset. He went into the town and, after drinking, he got into a fight.'

'What? Is he all right?'

'Yes, Ma. He's fine, but I hope he won't get into bother again.'

'Has he a job yet?'

'He spends his time helping John out with some secret project. I've persuaded him to look for a proper job in Derry, like Colleen. He told me he'll look for one when spring has ended.'

'How's Colleen getting on, Mary,' Bridget asked, pouring the tea.

'She's grand, Ma. She started a new job in a lawyer's office in the city. It seems if she does well the first few years they will train her to be a lawyer.'

'About time one of our family had a decent job!' Bridget scolded, sitting down beside Mary.

Mary took a deep breath. 'Did Thomas tell you about his next adventure?'

'I don't want to hear of any more adventures,' Bridget said crossly. 'The man needs to rest himself.'

'He's been asked to stand as our MP at the next election.'

There was complete silence in the room as everyone tried to take in what Mary had just said.

Bridget put turf into the stove and Rose took another sip of tea.

Thomas was in the stable giving hay to the horses when Michael came in behind him.

'They're looking good, Da,' Michael said quietly. 'You look after them very well.'

Thomas turned and looked at the young son who had grown into a very fit young man of twenty.

'Come to help, Son?' Thomas replied, smiling at him.

'My project with John is finished now, Da, so I'll have more time to help you.'

'So when am I going to see this project, Michael?'

'Very soon. John and I will give you plenty of notice,' he smiled.

'Life's going to get very busy for me soon. Maybe Ma has told you I am going to go into politics.'

Michael inched his way into the stable beside the horse and stroked his head. 'It's a very strange coincidence, Da, that we're both becoming interested in local issues at the same time.'

Thomas stopped working and looked up at his son. 'What do you mean?'

'I've joined a local group in Moville who want to campaign for Ireland to have self governance. We need to break free from London.

'What group?' Thomas asked, tensely.

'They call themselves 'The Fenians.'

Thomas was now about to explode but instead he slammed the fork against the stable wall and tried hard to control his feelings. 'I'm going to stand for the Liberal Party which aims to bring about greater self governance for Ireland, but the difference is that we will be doing this peacefully. The group that you want to join wants to bring about the same thing, but they're committed to doing it with violence!'

Michael now knew he was in trouble with his Da so tried to tone down what he was about to say.

'Not violence. Da. Just protests and demonstrations. We believe that the only way the English government will listen is to rise up and make our voices heard.'

'Michael, what nonsense has got into your head and who are you spending your time with?' said Thomas. His voice was now beginning to rise.

'Just my friends in Moville, Da. They're really good people.'

Thomas came round and took his son by the shoulders, looking closely into his face.

'Look at me Michael. That group has already got a bad reputation, and if you join them you are heading for big trouble. What starts off as protest can lead to violence very quickly. The reason I'm going to try and become an MP is to change things peacefully and, believe me, having seen the way things got out of hand in America, it's a far better way.'

'I need something of purpose to do, Da, just like you.' Michael dropped his eyes to the ground.

Thomas put his arm around his shoulders. 'You are a great son, Michael, and the right purpose will come to you soon, but this isn't the way you want to go, that's for certain. Now lets take these two horses for a ride.'

Michael moved to lift one of the saddles for his horse when he turned back to his da. 'I heard that you paid for Charity to go and leave me, Da,' he said, sounding hurt.

'I would never do that, Son. She had saved all the money she was supposed to spend on her wedding clothes. That paid her way to Spain. I gave her money for the ship journey from Spain to Africa. It was her choice, Michael. I would never encourage anyone to run away.'

'Am I suppose to wait so that some day she will decide she doesn't fit in with her own people and come running back to Ireland?'

'When you let go of something that you love, Son, it will return to you - if it's God's will for you.'

'Well if God has anything to do with my life he has a strange way of showing it.'

Thomas looked sad as he climbed onto his horse. 'Let's go for a race over the fields.'

William came out of his office and dropped an envelope onto Colleen's desk. 'Can you take that to the office of the business partnership in Bishop Street, please, and make sure that David Burns gets it.' He walked out the front door.

'He's in a grumpy mood today,' the secretary said under her breath.

'I know. He's still trying to work out a case that was supposed to go to court. I found a problem with it, which means he may have to pay his client a considerable amount of money himself.'

'Was that the proposed sale of the Waterside factory?'

'Yes. It has a small piece of ground attached to it that we missed which belongs to another man.'

'It'll be all right Colleen. All he has to do is to persuade the wee man to sell it and all will be well.'

'You know about it then?' Colleen asked surprised.

'I know about most things, young lady. You might do well to ask me occasionally.'

'I will Elaine. Thank you.' Colleen grabbed her coat and walked out onto the street.

It was a nice day for a walk as it had been unusually hot in Ireland that April. She enjoyed the walk from Clarendon Street to Bishop Street as she got to look into all the shop windows. She walked up and down Bishop street a few times looking for the office till she found a single doorway with the small sign, The Business Partnership. Colleen rang the bell and a young lady opened the door and invited her in. The office was small but decorated and furnished with very expensive taste.

'I would like to speak to David Burns please,' she said as she sat on the soft, red, leather couch.

The girl disappeared for a minute and then came back followed by a gentleman. Colleen nearly choked when she saw who it was. It was the man who had saved her life some months back! She just stared at him blankly nearly forgetting what she was there for.

'Ah. We meet again,' the man laughed 'Only this time in a safer environment.' He came straight over to shake her hand. Colleen was so shocked she almost stumbled as she tried to stand up. The man took her hand and helped her to her feet. 'Please, may I help you?'

'You already have,' Colleen blurted out with her cheeks blushing. 'I mean...in the past...when I was being careless.'

'Please, come into my office, miss. Would you like a cup of tea?'

'Emm...no. I'm fine, thank you. My boss asked me to deliver this envelope to you personally.'

'I see. And who would your boss be?'

'William McFarland, sir,' Colleen replied nervously.

'Ah. You must be the new legal assistant he has taken on. May I wish you well in your new post.'

'Thank you very much, sir. I hope I will meet his high standards.'

The gentleman asked her to take a seat opposite his by his desk. 'May one ask the name of this new lawyer in training.'

'Well, I'm not that far yet, sir. My name is Colleen.'

'That's a pretty name - for a very pretty young lady.'

Colleen blushed and moved nervously in the chair.

David opened the envelope and scanned the documents quickly. 'That's good news, Colleen.

Please thank your boss for putting this through so quickly.'

He stood up from his desk. 'If I may not interest you in tea, then at least let me walk you back to Clarendon Street. I would be afraid of you getting run over by a carriage again,' he smiled.

Colleen was now embarrassed and felt herself blushing. She had never met a more handsome man - and now he was offering to walk with her. She stood up. 'Thank you, sir, but I'm sure I will manage to walk that distance without harming myself,' she laughed nervously.

David came around beside her. 'I'm not sure about that, Colleen,' he smiled. 'On this sunny day it would be my honour to escort you. That is, if you don't mind.'

He opened the office door and Colleen could see that he wouldn't take no for an answer.

'Are you enjoying working for my friend, Miss Colleen?' he asked, walking towards the city centre.

'I am, actually. The job is fascinating and I am so grateful he offered it to me.' Colleen tried to keep up with his fast pace.

'William must have been watching you as he wouldn't offer jobs like that to just anyone.'

'He knows my parents as they are his clients.'

They crossed over the road and started walking down Shipquay Street when Colleen stopped suddenly. 'This is where you saved my life, David' she said.

'Oh I think that's slightly dramatic, Colleen. The horse might have knocked you to one side but I'm sure you would have been fine.'

'That is not what it looked like from my view from the ground,' she laughed.

David held out his arm for her to link with him as the hill was steep. 'May I ask where you are from Colleen.'

'My folks are from Donegal, but I am hoping to find myself a house near the city so I don't have to travel in a coach every day.'

'I'll see what I can do for you then. My family own a lot of property throughout the country.'

They talked all the way to Clarendon Street till they got to her office.

'It was very kind of you to walk me to my office, David. May I repay you some time?'

'Indeed young lady. You may repay me by letting me buy you lunch some day. There's a new department store just open in The Diamond called Austins and their restaurant is top class.'

'I will look forward to that, so good day to you.' Colleen felt like she was walking on air.

As she walked into her office, Elaine was standing in the middle of the room with a look of shock on her face. 'Was that David Burns you were talking to?'

'Yes,' said Colleen as she took her jacket off and hung it up on the coat stand.

'Do you know who he is?'

'He's a very nice, handsome gentleman who walked me all the way from his office to ours. That's all I know' Colleen smiled.

'He's the son of the wealthiest family in the north west, They own a huge amount of the city properties and control nearly everything that happens here!'

Colleen went very quiet. She stared down at the floor before hurrying into her own office.

'He's ten years older than you as well.' Elaine shouted after her, with a jealous tone in her voice.

The journey home that evening was interesting as her boss, William, was on the same coach. She decided to talk to him once he had put away his daily newspaper.

'My father has wanted to start a business of some kind in Derry, sir. There was a mysterious fire in the first one he tried. Would you have any suggestions?' Colleen asked, looking at him directly.

William paused for some time then slowly answered. 'Young lady, there is something that you need to learn about the city you are working in. Let me put this in the kindest way I can, without offending you. The city has a long tradition of being owned and run by people from Protestant background. They own most of the properties and businesses and have done so for a very long time. It's changing slowly as more people come from Donegal and even further away to find work. There are now a few shops that are owned by people from Catholic background. If your father wants to start a business in the city he will have a harder struggle than people from Protestant background.'

'My parents have a mixed marriage, sir. My father was from Catholic background and my mother from Protestant but neither of them hold to their traditions very well. They just see themselves as Christian people, and that's it.

'I am aware of that, Colleen. As you know, I am their lawyer, but if your father had met me before he tried to start a business I would have put him in touch with David Burns.'

Colleen nearly fell off the seat. 'Is that David Burns who I delivered an envelope to today?' she asked.

'Yes. David works for his father who owns a very large part of the city centre. He leaves most of the day-to-day decisions up to his son now as he is getting on in years.'

'David looks very young to have that responsibility.'

William looked at Colleen and suddenly realised that she was more than interested. 'He's about thirty, I think.' He smiled, and Colleen quickly looked out the window at the sea.

Chapter 6

Thomas tied his horse to the rail outside a very dingy looking pub in Moville. It was seven in the evening, and the town centre was already quiet after a busy fair day. 'What am I doing?' he thought to himself, as he walked slowly in the swing door. The bar was quiet and only had two men sitting on stools by the counter. The large barman pointed to a door at the back of the room and grunted, 'In there, if you're here for the meeting.'

The room was full of smoke and the smell of beer and Thomas waved his hand to brush the smoke away from his face. Six people were sitting at an old wooden table which was covered in bottles and glasses.

'Good evening, Thomas,' one of the men said, as he stood up and motioned to Thomas to join him at the far end of the table. Thomas didn't reply. He felt like walking out again. 'Sorry about the premises, but this is all we could find at short notice.'

Thomas sat down beside the man, who handed him a pile of papers. He then started to make a short speech. 'Gentlemen, in case any of you are not familiar with this gentleman, may I introduce you to Mr. Thomas Sweeney. He has agreed, in principle, to be our next candidate in the forthcoming election.' The men all cheered and some raised a glass. 'We are all here tonight to answer questions that Mr. Sweeney might have and to plan our strategy for the election.'

An hour later, with his eyes smarting from the smoke, Thomas said goodnight and promised them he would have an answer for them in a week's time when he had studied the manifesto.

It was dark when he left the pub and he was about to get on his horse when he noticed Michael's horse further up the street. He looked around and the street which was empty, apart from a man leading a donkey down the hill towards the harbour, and crept quietly towards Michael's horse. He came to the house and tried to see in the window without being seen. Just then a man appeared behind him. 'Are you looking for the meeting?' the man asked.

'Not sure if I am in the right place, thank you,' Thomas replied, trying not to sound nervous. 'What meeting is this anyway?'

'The Fenians meeting - and you are...?' He seemed annoyed.

'I was looking for my son, Michael Sweeney,' Thomas said quietly.

'I'll tell him you're here, then,' the man said, moving towards the door.

'No, please. Don't disturb him! It's just that I saw his horse here and wondered what he was doing. I'm away home now. I'll see him later.'

Thomas turned and walked back down the path while the man watched him leave.

It rained the next day and everyone commented how unusual the hot dry spell had been for the whole month of April. Thomas was in the kitchen eating one of Mary's scones while looking at the election manifesto. He was quiet, and Mary said nothing, watching him read.

'It's surprisingly good, Mary,' Thomas started. 'For a bunch of land men, this actually makes a lot of sense. These policies would be very good for Ireland. I just wonder if The Liberal Party can unseat such a strong Conservative Party right across England.'

'If you were to stand, Thomas, and even get elected, how much time would you have to spend in London?' Mary asked, pouring more tea for Thomas.

'That's the big question, my love. I 'll make contact with a friend of mine who's already an MP down the country. I'm sure he'll know.'

'Michael was very late coming home again last night and he's still in bed. 'Mary said, annoyed. 'I don't like him going to the town at night.'

Thomas said nothing.

A while later, right out of the blue, Mary asked, 'What happened in England? You never told me.'

Thomas was quiet for a while before answering carefully. 'Strange Mary. A young lady appeared one night at Richard's door and said she was the daughter of Lord Shrewsbury. She said that her French mother was a nanny to Christina and Edward. Shrewsbury was had an affair with her and she got pregnant so he paid her a huge some of money to get rid of her.'

'Do you believe this, Thomas? It sounds like a made-up story.'

'I would have thought that too, Mary, but for one thing. She is like an identical twin to Christina - and she gave me some shock when I saw her!'

'How could she be identical to Christina with a different mother?' Mary asked, as she sat down opposite Thomas, looking very concerned.

'I'm still trying to work that one out Mary. It doesn't make sense; yet she's very convincing. When I first walked into the room and saw her I thought Christina had come back from the grave! Not only does she look like her but she talks and walks like her as well.'

'Is there any way of proving her story?'

'Richard and his lawyer friend are looking into it and we hope to hear back soon. If Christina was still alive she would be forty five. This woman looks younger, but then I was never very good at guessing people's ages.'

Just then Michael came down the stairs.

'Where were you last night, Michael?' Mary asked sharply.

'Just in the town with my friends, Ma.' He went over and poured himself a cup of tea.

'Why would you be out so late with friends when there's nothing open at that time of night?'

'We usually just sit and talk, Ma.' Michael was nervous and kept looking at his Da to say something. Thomas never looked up.

'It's not safe riding the horse along the road in the dark, Son. You need to come home earlier.'

Thomas got up from his papers, folded them away and walked out. 'I'm away to see John.'

Thomas had nearly reached John's house in Moville when Sergeant O'Hare came riding towards him on his big black horse.

'Good day, Thomas. How are you?' he called.

Thomas turned his horse to join him on the other side of the road. 'I'd be very well, Alfred, if only the people here would give me a bit of peace,' he joked.

Alfred laughed. 'It's hard to keep anything secret in this wee town. I heard that you might be going to stand as our MP.'

'So I'm told. It would seem that I have very little choice if I ever want to enjoy my retirement.'

'I think you would do well, Thomas. After all the adventures you have been through I would think parliament in London will seem like a boys' club to you.'

'We shall see. Anyway, how do you like your new job?'

'It is very interesting - compared to New York. Trying to sort out neighbourly disputes is a lot safer than trying to arrest armed gangs. Sure, there are no secrets here so no one can get away with anything,' he laughed.

'I wish you well, Alfred. Please call in for tea when you're passing.'

'One thing I was going to mention to you, Thomas,' Alfred adjusted his seat in the saddle, looking a bit uncomfortable. 'Em ... I just wanted to warn you ... your son, Michael, is keeping company with some people I wouldn't have much regard for right now.'

'Yes, The Fenians.'

'You know, then?'

'I followed him last night and could see he was at some kind of meeting,' Thomas said sounding concerned.

'I would try and persuade him not to become involved, Thomas. They want the same ideals for Ireland as your Liberal Party, but they want to make it happen sooner - and with violence. They are not good men and I'd be very concerned that he ends up getting into a lot of trouble.'

'Thank you, Alfred. I'll speak to him again, but he's twenty now so it's hard to keep in hand.'

Alfred went to move his horse. 'If you want I could have a word with him. That might scare him.'

Thomas pulled his horse round to ride on. 'Thanks Sergeant. I may call on you to do that.'

Richard was playing with his children by the fountain at the front of the house. They were splashing water at each other when Ann came down the steps behind them. 'Richard,' she called. 'Andrew's about to leave for the day and he was wondering if he could talk to you.'

'As long as you take over soaking the girls.' Richard replied, laughing, as he splashed more water over his children much to their delight.

'Back shortly' he waved, as he climbed the steps.

Andrew, the house manager, came out of the front door and met Richard at the top of the steps.

'Hello Andrew. What can I do for you on this fine day?' Richard sat on the wall and motioned for him to join him.

'I've been a butler, and now a house manager, here in this house for forty five years, sir,' he started, with his head down

'Goodness. Please don't say you're leaving,' Richard interrupted.

'Ah, no sir. I hope that day will be a while yet - though I am sixty five now.'

'I wish I was as young looking as you Andrew,' Richard replied, kindly.

'I wish to talk to you about a delicate matter, sir. First let me tell you this. In my time serving Lord Shrewsbury, and then Thomas, and now your kind self, I have never broken confidence. It was something I was taught in training, but also learnt out of the greatest respect for the owners of this house.'

Richard moved forward on his seat as he wasn't sure what was coming next. Andrew looked nervous.

'The young lady called Simone, sir, who has recently joined the house...' he paused.

'Go on, Andrew. I'm listening.'

'Her name is not Simone.'

Richard stood up and stared at Andrew. 'What?'

'Her name is Caroline. She's named after her real mother who was Lady Caroline Shrewsbury.'

'What are you saying Andrew?' Richard was almost shouting.

'This is where I must break confidence for the first time in my life and I hope that you will pardon me. I overheard Simone telling you that her French mother, who was called Renee, was sent away by Lord Shrewsbury when she became pregnant from an affair with him. This is not the case, sir. The true story is extremely hard for anyone to believe or understand, but I must tell it to you now.'

Richard sat down beside Andrew again and was now more gentle as he could see he was very upset at telling his story.

'When Lady Shrewsbury was giving birth upstairs here in the house she was attended by our local doctor and nurse. This was because she had not been well during the pregnancy. Caroline Shrewsbury had not just physical problems, if you know what I mean. When the first baby, Christina, was born, the doctor was shocked to find out there was a second baby in her womb. When the baby was delivered, the doctor immediately had concerns as it was very blue, and not breathing. It took the doctor some time to get the baby to cry by patting it on the its back. Lady Shrewsbury was horrified and screamed for them to take it away. The first baby was placed in her arms while the nurse took the second one out of the room.

Two weeks passed, and the situation got worse. Lady Shrewsbury seemed to be having some kind of breakdown and she wasn't even well enough to look after Christina. Lord Shrewsbury called the doctor and I heard them having a long chat in the living room. It seems that Lady Shrewsbury was demanding that they put the second baby up for adoption as she didn't want two babies.

After a month Lady Shrewsbury was still in bed and everyone was distraught. She wouldn't even look at the second child or acknowledge that she was hers. The French nanny, Renee, eventually stepped in and offered to raise the baby as her own. By this stage the baby was quite normal. There were days of discussion with the doctor and friends and the outcome was that Lord Shrewsbury, with great sadness, agreed to send Renee and his daughter Caroline, who they named after his wife, to live in Manchester. She was bought a huge house and paid a very large sum of money. Until the day he died in that terrible accident, he kept it secret. I was the only person who knew the truth, and he swore me to secrecy. I have kept it a secret till today as I felt you and Thomas should know who you are looking after.'

Richard stood and stared at the butler as if he just heard the greatest fairytale of all time. 'This is beyond belief, Andrew. If anyone else in the world had just told me this story I would now be laughing in their face. As it has come from you I am in great shock and don't know what to say.'

'I feel like I should resign now, sir, as I have broken confidence, and that I have never done before in my entire life,' Andrew said sadly, standing up to face Richard. 'I will work till you find a replacement for me.'

'Don't be ridiculous, Andrew. You have not broken confidence. You have just set Caroline free for a whole new life. Thomas and I are indebted to you for telling us the truth. We couldn't understand how Simone, who is now Caroline, could possibly look so like Christina if she had not come from the same mother and father. It was just a mystery to us.' Richard walked in a circle at the top of the steps. 'I must tell Thomas.'

Andrew moved to walk away. 'Please don't say anything to anyone, Andrew, till we inform Simone and get the legal things sorted.'

'One other thing, Richard,' Andrew paused. 'If you find any of my story to hard to believe, may I suggest that you unlock Lord Shrewsbury's room upstairs. It has been locked since he died. Thomas did not want anyone to use it. I would say that somewhere in his office you will find the birth certificate of both his daughters, which will prove my story is true.'

'We shall do that tomorrow, Andrew, if Thomas can remember where he put the key.'

'I have the key, sir.' Andrew looked very guilty.

'I see, Andrew. Well, let's not trouble ourself about this till tomorrow. Enjoy the rest of your day off. Tomorrow we will open the office.' Richard patted Andrew on the back and then turned and walked down the steps. He was deeply troubled as he felt no one would believe such a crazy story.

'You look very pale, Richard' Ann said, as she lifted her daughter down from the fountain. 'Are you ill?'

'No, Ann. I'm not ill but I have just been told a story which is so ridiculous it can only be true.' He sat down by the water and stared at the fountain. 'I shall tell you later, my love, when we're on our own.'

Chapter 7

Thomas was very quiet over breakfast. He had a lot on his mind today and had some big decisions to make. Mary sat down opposite him. 'Have you found out how long each session will last in London yet?'

'Not yet, Mary. It's something I'll have to consider carefully before I make a final decision.'

He got up from the table and sighed, 'I think I'll walk to John's house today. I need time to think.' He headed for the door and Mary called after him. 'Pray about it, Thomas.'

Thomas was about to walk onto the main Moville road when Seamus, the postman, came round the corner in his post wagon. 'Good day, Thomas. I was about to call at your house,' he said, as he opened his bag. 'Another telegram from England for you, sir.'

He went over and collected it from him. 'Thanks Seamus. You might be getting a few of these in the near future.'

Thomas quickly opened it as he walked towards the town. 'I'm coming to Ireland tomorrow!' the telegram read, briefly. It was from Richard. 'What now?' thought Thomas, as he scrunched the paper and put it in his pocket. It took him nearly an hour to reach John's house as he enjoyed walking slowly in the light rain. John was walking his horse by the front door.

'Well, you are sight!' he laughed, as Thomas approached him, soaking wet.

'Needed to think, John.'

'Oh dear that's very dangerous, sir,' he joked. 'Any time you think, it usually causes trouble.'

'You are the one to blame this time. I've decided to agree to the position as MP, once I find out about the schedule.'

'Good on ya', boy.' John came over and shook hands.

'On one condition, my friend.' Thomas looked passed him at his house. 'You will have to help me.'

John pulled the horse round and tied the rains to a tree.

'What made you come to your decision, Thomas?'

Thomas sighed and looked down at the ground. 'Michael joining The Fenians. I thought that if I don't do something positive I can hardly tell him not to become involved with a group that basically wants the same as I do.'

'Yes, but not the same way.' John looked serious for a moment.

'Did you get talking to him?'

'I did, but he has made up his mind that he wants to do the same as you. He's convinced this group will make a difference.'

'Did you try to get him to see sense?'

'I did, Thomas. He did say he would back off for a while till he sees how you get on. Maybe you could take him on as an assistant.'

'That's a very good idea. Let me have a good think about that, now.'

John tried to lighten the conversation. 'A long time ago you asked me to think about a business that might do well in Derry.'

'Not sure, any more. My first attempt ended in disaster when the building burnt down.' Thomas went over and stroked John's horse. 'I don't know if I want to try again.'

'They found out that that fire was actually an accident. You shouldn't let that put you off trying again.'

'The city seems well catered for in business and is heavily controlled by a small number of people.'

'Buttons!' John announced suddenly.

Thomas looked curiously at him. What was he saying? 'Buttons to you too,' he retorted, foolishly.

'No, I'm serious Thomas. Buttons.'

'Have you been making more poitín, John, or just lost your sanity?'

'The city is full of shirt factories, and a huge new one is being built at the bottom of Abercorn Road. Derry's becoming one of the biggest shirt and suit manufactures in the whole of the country and is already exporting shirts to America. So think about it, Thomas. What do you need for shirts?'

Thomas just stared at him, waiting for the answer.

'Buttons. Every shirt and jacket needs buttons, and at present all the buttons are being imported from England, and even further away.'

Thomas screwed up his face. 'We know nothing about buttons. That would be a huge gamble.'

'Over the last six months I've taken it upon myself to do some research and even went to a button factory in Dublin pretending to be a client. I reckon it wouldn't be a huge gamble at all. With modern machinery we could be supplying all the factories in Derry and beyond in a very short time.'

Thomas walked round to sit down on the garden seat. 'I'm about to try and enter politics. How could I give my time to starting a new crazy venture with buttons?'

'Richard could,' John smiled, '... with your money. He could set it up and run it for you, and maybe even give Michael a job.'

Thomas looked thoughtfully at the ground for a minute and then, looking up, 'I'm not sure, but right now would you mind getting your trap and leaving me home? I'm tired of this rain.'

Colleen was working her way through a pile of legal documents pertaining to a new case they had taken on. She didn't hear the front door open. Elaine came into her office a few moments later.

'This came by personal delivery for you.' She smiled as she threw a pink envelope down on her desk. Colleen took no notice of it at first as she was deeply engrossed in a document she was reading. When she finished reading she suddenly looked down at the envelope and stared at it. She knew all envelopes delivered to the office were either brown or white. This was the first pink one she had seen. She lifted it up and examined it as if it was about to explode. Her hand began to shake a little as she opened it carefully with her gold knife, realising who it was from.

'I'm very hungry today and am going to the new Austins Restaurant. Would you like to join me for lunch? David.'

Colleen had to read the words several times before it sunk in. She took the note and cooled her face down by waving it in front her. Sitting quietly at her desk for a few minutes, she considered carefully how she would respond.

'When did this come, Elaine?' she asked softly.

'Just now, Colleen, hand delivered by a young girl.'

Elaine read the note.

What will I do?, Colleen asked, nervously.

Elaine read it a few times more and then laughed. 'What will you do? What sort of question is that? You have just been asked on a lunch date by the most eligible bachelor in Ireland and you're asking me what you should do? Are you crazy?'

Colleen stood there like a fourteen year old and moved her hands nervously. 'I've never been on a date before,' she said, nervously.

'Look. sweetie. It's just lunch. He hasn't asked you to marry him!' Elaine came round and put her arm around Colleen's shoulders. 'Just look at it as a chance to eat in a fabulous new restaurant. You can just look at it as a chance to get to know each other.'

Colleen turned and gave Elaine a hug. 'Thank you, Elaine. You're a good friend.'

She turned and went back into her office. Walking over to big mirror tucked away in the corner she examined her face closely and looked down at her dull dress with dismay. What on earth did he see in her to want to ask her out?

David was waiting at the entrance to the new department store. Shoppers were going in and out the front door in droves eager to try out the very first department store in the world. Many people talked to him, as he was one of the best known people in the city.

Colleen was so nervous she walked behind a couple almost wishing she had stayed in the office.

David saw her as she crossed Ferryquay Street and waved. Why was her heart beating so fast? This was the man who had saved her life. Perhaps he just wanted to be friends.

David took her hand and kissed it. 'I'm so glad you came, Colleen. I wasn't sure if you would.'

Colleen blushed, and replied nervously, 'Now how could I turn down an invitation to such a splendid new place?'

David took her by the arm and escorted her into the shop and to the grand stairs. 'Have you ever been in this store before?' He asked, smiling.

'No, it looks amazing,' Colleen said looking all around her.

'The restaurant has amazing views of the city,' David said, leading Colleen by the arm up the stairs.

He escorted to a reserved table by the window. 'What do think?'

Colleen was in shock as she stood looking out the window. 'I have never been this high up before. Look at the view! I can see all the way down the river!' She stood with her hands held up to her face.

David pulled out her chair and motioned for her to sit down. Colleen looked like she was about to cry.

'Are you all right, Colleen?' David asked with concern.

'I'm sorry. No one has ever done anything like this for me before. This is so amazing. Thank you so much.'

David took the menu from the waiter and placed it in front of Colleen, realising she was slightly overwhelmed.

'May I suggest the roast beef? It's the best I have ever had.'

Colleen looked at the menu and then placed it to one side. 'Listen, David,' Colleen started slowly.

'I know you live here in the big city with high society, and you probably have any amount of high society girls chasing after you. I'm just a simple country girl who was brought up to value people as I find them. I just wanted you to know that.' She blushed and didn't know where to look. She immediately regretted her sudden outburst.

David just looked at her and smiled for a few seconds before he replied. 'I'm so glad you told me that, but I had already guessed that anyhow.' He paused and poured Colleen a glass of water.

'Yes, you're right, Colleen. I live in 'high society' as you call it, and yes, I've had quite a number of young ladies - all after my money, I might add. However, you might be shocked to learn that is not me. My father is the wealthiest man in this part of the country but my mother is from the country. It is she who taught me to treat people the same way as you do. I give money to people in need without anyone knowing.'

Colleen smiled so much she felt her cheeks would break. She stared at David and shook her head.

It was ridiculous, but she felt she was falling deeply in love with this man who she barely knew, sitting before her.

Their lunch arrived and the conversation lightened. David had her laughing about the times that they had met in the street. He knew in his heart from the minute he rescued Colleen in Shipquay Street that he had found someone very different. Every time she looked into his eyes he felt a burning in his chest. No girl had ever made him feel like this before.

'I would love to spend some time with you, Colleen. I believe we might have a lot in common.

'That would be great. Maybe you could come and visit us in Donegal,' she giggled.

'Sounds wonderful, Colleen. David stood up and reached for her hand to lead her to the stairs.

I would love to see what the store sells, David, so maybe I'll walk around each floor.'

'Then I'll leave you, young lady, to window shop on your way out. 'Till we meet again.' He kissed her hand again and bowed. Colleen nearly melted with the warmth she felt. She watched him walk down the stairs in front of her and stood staring, unaware of people passing.

'Can I help you, ma'am?' A man in a uniform said, as he walked over to her.

'Thank you, sir, but right now no one could help me.' She mumbled quietly, smiling, as she walked down the stairs.

Chapter 8

Thomas was standing in Moville town centre waiting for Richard's coach to arrive. A man on a bicycle stopped as he was passing. 'Mr. Sweeney, I heard the good news last night.' Thomas just looked at him and turned his head to one side. 'So glad you're going to stand as our next MP. I'll do everything I can to help you get elected.'

'Why would you do that? I don't think I've done that much for anyone in my town - at least not yet'

'Oh, if you only knew what you already did for hundreds of people here during the blight. People will never forget your kindness, Mr. Sweeney. My family owe you so much.'

'Thank you, sir. What's your name, by the way?'

'Colum Doherty.'

'Well, Colum. I'm not elected yet, but if I am then let me know if there's anything I can do for you.'

At that the coach arrived and Thomas bade him good day.

Richard jumped out of the coach and Thomas gave him a hug. 'I brought my trap here so we could talk on the way back to Greencastle.'

'Good idea, Thomas. It's better that you hear my news before you tell Mary.'

They both climbed up onto the front seat.

'This must be serious for you to travel all the way from England. Well, tell me, what has happened now?'

'Simone is not Simone,' Richard started, sounding anxious. He paused. 'She is your former sister-in-law, Caroline.'

Thomas stopped the trap and turned to Richard. 'What!' he shouted in disbelief.

'She's the twin sister of your late wife, Christina. She was named after her real mother, Lady Caroline Shrewsbury.'

Thomas went pale. 'No, Richard, that couldn't be possible! Are you sure?' He held his head in his hands.

'It's true, all right,' Richard said quietly. 'When Lady Shrewsbury gave birth to Christiana no one knew, including the doctor, that there was another baby. When the second baby was born she screamed and told them to take her away. Despite Lord Shrewsbury and the doctor trying to convince her, she refused to accept her as her own and demanded that the baby be taken away. This went on for weeks and her mental state started to deteriorate. A month later the French nanny, Renee, offered to raise the child as her own as she had fallen in love with the baby. Shrewsbury bought Renee a huge house outside Manchester. He then gave her an income for life to bring up the baby. It was only when her mother was dying that Caroline found out who her father really was.

That is, when she came to our house to see if any of her family were still alive.'

'So when I met Caroline it was like Christina had returned from the grave,' Thomas choked.

'Twins are so close they can feel each other's love and pain. That is what I felt for those few seconds. I felt that closeness, like Christina was there. It was very real Richard'

Richard put his arm around Thomas's shoulders. 'Please, my dearest friend. You let Christina go a long time ago. Christina is gone, Thomas. This is her twin sister.'

Thomas stared at Richard for some time before turning to start the trap again. 'This changes everything. How did you find this out?'

'Andrew, my chief butler told me. When he saw that we were going to bring Simone into the house he felt we needed to know the truth. We opened the lord's room upstairs and found the twins' birth certificates. I have them with me.'

'That room was never to be opened,' Thomas said sharply.

'I know, Thomas, but it was the only way we could get the proof for you.'

'That means she is Lady Caroline Shrewsbury - and now we must treat her so,' Thomas said firmly. 'Please don't tell my family this until I'm ready. I would like to see her again and talk with her myself.'

Michael was annoyed that his da's friend, Richard, was back again to stay. The last time he came he took up a lot of the time that Michael thought his da should be spending with him. He sneaked out after dinner saying he was going for a walk on the beach. Instead he walked down the driveway to the Main Road and, to avoid his parents knowing he had gone to Moville, he decided to walk the two miles. He was early for The Fenians' meeting, but went on into the run-down house and was surprised to see that Kieran, their leader, was already there on his own.

'Come on in, young Michael,' Kieran said, as he pushed a chair out for him. 'Where did you leave your horse?'

'No horse tonight. I didn't want my parents knowing that I was coming here. They're not pleased I have joined your group.'

'Let me tell you something, young fella, that might uprise you.' He pulled a chair out and sat down opposite Michael. 'I have great respect for your father. He has done more for local people than anyone in history. I'm told he is going to stand as the next MP for The Liberal

Party. I have the utmost admiration for what he's doing and hope he gets elected.'

'I thought we were against going down the political route, Kieran.' Michael looked surprised.

'Both directions must meet and go together Michael. Your father's party want the same as we do, basically. The difference is that they might take forty years or more to bring about an Ireland governed by itself. We believe that protests, and maybe even taking up arms, will make the English change sooner. So you see, both will go together, and there are ways we can help each other.'

'Why is my da so against me joining you then?'

'Like any father, he doesn't want his son getting hurt or in trouble with the law.'

'Could I get hurt, sir'?

'I hope not, son, There will be times in the future where we might have to defend ourselves, but hopefully it will never come to that.'

The other men started to arrive, and soon their meeting started. Michael was confused after speaking with his leader and he left before the meeting finished so he would be home for eight.

The sun was setting when he walked up his driveway, so he decided to walk on the beach where he used to walk with Charity. He kicked the sand as he watched the small waves lap onto the beach and began to think of the many happy times he had with her. Sitting down on a rock, he breathed in the fresh salt air.

Just then Martha appeared walking from the other direction. 'Hello my sweet nephew. How are you on this beautiful evening?'

Michael looked and smiled at Martha. 'Where's your family today?'

'John's putting them to bed. I thought I would see if there was anyone about this evening.'

Michael dropped his head and looked at the sand. 'My Charity left me just as we were going to have an amazing life together. Why, Martha? We loved each other so much, and shared so much fun and plans.'

Martha sat down beside him and took his hand her own. 'I'm a simple girl, Michael, so I see things in a simple way. Sometimes it makes no sense when life gets very complicated.'

Michael studied Martha carefully. She had the kindest face he had ever seen. 'I can't work anything out any more, Martha. My life is so empty.'

'When my da drowned I was only fourteen,' she said softly. 'He was the greatest da in the world. I was supposed to be slow at learning and it did take me longer to learn to speak and read than Mary. I loved my da and he always took me to the fields with him. He taught me how to work with the animals. He was my life really. Then he drowned, along with your granda. It seemed so unfair. Life was so empty without him. Then Mary left and I was on my own for three years. My ma never knew that I went to sleep every night crying. It was only when I prayed and asked God to help me that I realised that my da was still with me in everything he had taught me to do. I realised that God would want me to help others just like he helped me. So I did. Then, eventually, he brought me John, and now I help him.'

'I don't believe in God the way my parents do, Martha. I find they simplify things too easily.'

'In a way life is only complicated if you make it so, and that's why I like to keep my walk with God simple.' She stood up and walked towards the sea. 'If God took Charity away from you Michael, then He will either bring her back or bring someone else into your life. It's as simple as that.'

'I wish I had your faith, Martha.'

'You can. Just ask Him to help you believe, and He will.'

Richard was late down for breakfast the next day. Mary had kept him a big plate of soda scone bread, which he loved, and put an egg on the pan for him. Then he appeared, still looking troubled.

'So what important business brings our Richard to Ireland that a telegram wouldn't suffice?' Mary asked smiling.

'Thomas told you about the young girl who arrived at our door Mary, I presume?'

'He did, Richard and that she was the image of Christina. A very strange thing, indeed!'

'Well it's all true. I just came to tell Thomas that we have the proof that she is indeed entitled to the title of Lady Shrewsbury. There are some complications to her story, but I'll let Thomas tell you that in good time.'

'Seems very mysterious. Well, anyway, it was so good of you to travel all this way to tell him yourself.'

'Well you know, Mary, I wanted to check on our house here, as Ann and I would love to move back some day. Life is very stuffy over there - and I don't get any of your soda scone bread.'

'The house will always be waiting for you, and we frequently check up on it.'

'I would have to find a proper manager to look after the estate, after the mess the last man left. If I could find someone who would look after it properly then it would only be a matter of popping over there once or twice a year.'

'When are you heading back Richard?'

'Tomorrow morning. I'll get the seven o'clock coach to Derry and then the new train to Belfast.'

When Richard finished his breakfast he went looking for Thomas. He found him on his boat at the bottom of the garden. 'You didn't tell Mary yet,' he commented, as looked down at Thomas polishing a brass plate on his boat. 'Not yet,' he sighed. 'I need to take it all in myself first.'

Richard picked up a shell from the harbour and rubbed it in his hands. 'Look, Thomas. You are my greatest friend and I owe everything to you. That is why I never want to see you hurt again. When

Christina died I cried with you for a long time. When you married Mary and moved back to Ireland

I was so pleased for you. Now I am so worried for you. I'm afraid that the sight of Christina's identical twin will stir up sad memories in you that you had buried a long time ago.

'That won't happen, Richard. Once I get over the shock of her being like Christina she will just be a friend, who I must look after for her father's sake.'

Richard stared out to sea. 'I do hope so, Thomas' he sighed.

Thomas brightened up. 'I didn't tell you, Richard, that I'm going to stand for parliament in the next election in June. I expect I will be in London a lot of the time.'

'Good grief, Thomas! What on earth has got into your head now? I thought you were finished with adventures. That's the craziest thing I have heard you suggest yet.'

Thomas paused, climbing out of the boat, and came and stood in front of Richard.

'For a long time now I've wanted to see my wee island recover from its sadness and become the prosperous nation it deserves. The local people want me to serve them in London. I believe I can make a difference.'

'What are you running away from?' Richard asked, in a rare instance of bravery.

Thomas was shocked at his question and looked away at the sea. 'I'm not running away, Richard. What gives you that idea?'

'The routine at parliament means you will be away from home for three months of the year. Will Mary move to London with you?'

'Parliament starts in September and runs until Christmas. It starts again in January and ends in June, with a week off at Easter. Is that what you really want, my friend? You will hardly ever be at home.'

'I could come and stay with you in Shrewsbury.'

'Oh yes, where Simone will be living as Lady Caroline Shrewsbury. Come on, Thomas. You haven't thought this through, very well, I think.'

Thomas smiled at his friend and walked back towards the house. Richard threw the shell with force into the sea.

Colleen was talking to Elaine in the front office and they were giggling about her lunch with David. William walked in the front door. 'Colleen, a moment please.' She followed him quickly, turning to make eyes at Elaine.

'The factory case is ready for the courts and will be heard at ten am tomorrow. I'd like you to come with me as my legal assistant.'

Colleen stood in silence, not sure she heard right. 'I'm no lawyer, sir, and have never been in court in my life. I couldn't possibly be ready.'

'That is my decision, Colleen, and I'm quite convinced by your work that you are more than ready.'

'What would I have to do, sir?'

'Sit and look pretty as usual. Hand me documents at critical times and help me answer any questions that I might have trouble with.'

'Gosh, sir, that's some responsibility for me! I'm not even twenty yet.'

'You have made an enormous impression on David Burns. He thinks you are one of the brightest girls ever to come to this city. He told me that he can see you as a lawyer in no time.'

'Did he really say that, sir?' Colleen blushed.

'That's settled then, girl. I need to go over these papers with you. I hope you aren't in a hurry home.'

The next morning Colleen was feeling very anxious as she travelled on the early coach to the city. She had gone over and over the files with William till she knew the arguments off by heart. It was a very simple case and should be cleared up in one day. She was surprised the claimant even brought the case and they had no hope of winning. Walking up Shipquay Street, she was surprised to see how many shops were open at that time of the morning. When she got to The Court House in Bishop Street she suddenly felt like running home. The impressive white building with a British flag flying made it look very scary to her. She had never seen such an impressive building and the thought of entering as an assistant lawyer nearly brought her to tears.

'So glad you could make it, Colleen,' said a voice from behind her. She turned and was shocked to see David standing behind her, smiling.

'David, I'm so glad to see you,' she stuttered. 'But why are you here?'

'You are helping in my defence,' he laughed, taking her arm, and headed to the court house door.

'Excuse me, I don't understand.' Colleen almost cried.

'The man is trying to sue my company.'

'Is City Enterprises your company? William never told me.'

'Mmm...I asked him not to let you know. I suppose that was very naughty of me,' he smiled.

Colleen looked at him and wanted to hug him and punch him at the same time. 'This is my first time in a court so I'm very glad you and William are with me.'

David turned and faced her, taking both her hands. 'I'm afraid you are on your own, Colleen.'

Colleen's colour drained from her face and she thought she was going to be sick. 'What do you mean 'I'm on my own'?'

'William will not be in court.'

'Why won't he be in court?' She was ready to explode.

'He has been called away to Belfast to a big criminal trial. He's left this case in your capable hands.'

'No,' Colleen shouted. She then realised people in the court could hear her. 'I can't do this.'

David put his hands on her shoulders and looked her straight in the eye. 'Listen, Colleen, all you have to do is to remember to address the judge as 'your honour' and go through the notes, as you did last night.'

'You and William planned this.' She was getting angry.

'We wouldn't have planned this if we had the slightest doubt that you could do it.' David leaned forward and kissed her on her forehead.

He led her into the court room and showed her where to sit, then sat down beside her.

'What are all these people doing here?' Colleen asked nervously.

'They're just here to see you,' David laughed.

Colleen pinched him on the sleeve. 'I can't do this, David. I'm not a lawyer.'

'Oh yes you can. You'll be great.'

Suddenly a court clerk shouted 'All rise! Justice Harrison presiding.'

The judge walked in and took his seat. Everyone sat down.

'In the matter between George Dixon and City Enterprises.' The judge read out, 'A claim on a disputed purchase. Who is representing the claimant'?

A tall well dressed gentleman stood up and replied 'I am, Your Honour. Colin Harper.'

'And who is standing for the defendant?' The judge looked down at Colleen.

'I am Your Majesty,' Colleen blurted out as she stood up quickly. 'Colleen Sweeney.'

The courtroom burst into laughter till the judge banged his hammer.

'Order in the court.' The judge looked down at a very frightened Colleen. 'I have been called many things in this courtroom, young lady, but never 'Your Majesty'. 'Your Honour' will do me fine.'

The judge put his hand over his face to hide his smile. 'Go ahead, Mr. Harper.'

'Your honour our case is very straightforward,' Harper began. 'My client purchased a substantial building which he was going to turn into a factory. It was only when he applied for permission to the city authorities that he discovered that a section of the two acre sight belonged to another owner. The authorities could not, therefore, give permission for any development until this was sorted out. When my client approached the owner of the land, the gentleman refused to sell it, therefore rendering the whole purchase useless to my client. What's more, your honour, my client's legal company failed to see this when they were processing the deeds, so we are looking for compensation from both of the defendants if they cannot agree responsibility.'

'I see,' the judge said, as he turned to Colleen.

'Would the defendants have any explanation for this error of judgement and how they might be willing to compensate the claimant?'

Colleen got to her feet and mumbled a few words. 'Speak up young lady. I can't hear you.'

'Your Honour, I am somewhat puzzled as to why this case has actually been brought before you, sir.'She paused. Her hand was shaking so much that the papers she was holding fell to the floor. She picked them up and looked at David who gave her a thumbs up signal.

'It might have served Mr. Harper and his client better if they had bothered to consult with my company first before taking legal action, as we have the deeds to the piece of land in question and there is no dispute as to who now owns it.

'Really?' The judge looked cross. 'Can you prove this, young lady - I mean, Miss Sweeney?'

'Yes, Your Honour. I have the deeds with me.' Colleen shuffled through the papers that were now mixed up after falling on the floor. She eventually found the paper and held it up.

'Approach the bench, please,' the judge ordered.

Colleen smiled at Mr. Harper as she walked passed him to reach the judge.

The judge studied the document for a few minutes and was very quiet, until he announced.

'This is a very clear legal title to this piece of land and it's in the claimant's name.' Looking over his glasses at Harper, he said, 'You would do well, sir, in future, to check your facts before wasting the court's time. Case dismissed!' He banged his hammer and rose up from his seat and walked out.

'Congratulations! You have just won your first case,' David said, shaking hands with Colleen.

She was not impressed and grabbed the pile of notes, scurrying towards the door. David followed her to the street. She turned to him crossly. 'That was a set up,' she said in anger.

'Not exactly, when we knew we would win,' David laughed, with a big smile on his face.

'William knew this would happen, and that's why he sent me. It was nothing to do with my skill, and if anyone finds out that I'm not a lawyer I could go to jail.'

Colleen walked off in a rage leaving David shaking his head and smiling. She had got to the end of Bishop Street when a very expensive coach pulled up beside her and David called to her. 'May I give my favourite lawyer a lift? It's going to rain.'

Colleen was about to say no when her heart got the better of her. She couldn't resist David's dark, sparkling eyes and broad smile.

Saying nothing, she climbed into the most luxurious coach she had ever seen, The soft seats were made of blue velvet and there were dark red curtains at the side of each window. She couldn't help notice that the internal door handle was gold, as were the trimmings above the seats.

Colleen sat opposite David, but stared out the window as the coach moved down Shipquay Street.

'I must apologise, Colleen. I didn't think this would upset you. William thought it would be an easy introduction to the court. You were actually amazing and spoke like an accomplished lawyer.'

Colleen was silent for a while and then turned and smiled at David. 'So accomplished I called the judge 'Your Majesty'!'

'In my years of attending his court I have never seen him laugh, until to day. That was a great achievement.' David leant over and took her hand in his. 'I believe you have a great career ahead of you.'

The coach turned left onto The Strand Road and it wasn't long before they reached her office.

'I was thinking that, as you did so well today, I might drive you home in my coach.'

'Thank you, David, but it's only mid-day and I have to finish work,' she replied, as she went to open the door. David stopped her. 'Give me a second,' he said, as he jumped out of the coach.

He returned a minute later and jumped back into the coach. 'William has given you the rest of the day off.'

'William's in Belfast at another case,' she said suspiciously. 'Who were you talking to?'

David just sat back and smiled.

'This is a disgrace! I mean, I must have been stupid not to have seen through this from the start.' She shook her head and then gave a cheeky smile.

David opened the window, leaned out, and called to the driver. 'Greencastle in Donegal, please, driver.'

'What a wonderful house you live in, Colleen.' David said, as the coach drew up outside the front door. 'May I ask what your father does to live in such a place?'

'He has a six thousand acre estate that he inherited in England so he doesn't do very much now at all.'

'You have your own harbour and boat, Colleen. I'm very impressed. Will I be allowed to meet your parents or are you still cross with me?'

'How could anyone be cross with you?' she blurted out and then realised what she said and blushed.

Just then Thomas and Richard came out of the house and looked with admiration at the coach.

Colleen introduced them to David and then went into the house. She asked Mary if she could invite David for dinner before coming back out to find the three men were getting on so well and were deep in conversation. She went back inside.

Chapter 9

Richard was up at six thirty for breakfast the next morning to catch the seven o'clock coach to Derry. He was sitting chatting to Mary over his tea and toast when Thomas came down the stairs holding a small bag.

'Where are you going Thomas?' Richard asked.

'With you to England,' Thomas replied, winking at Mary.

Richard was silent and not looking happy at the plan. 'I think I can manage this situation quite well on my own,' he said firmly.

I am quite sure you can Richard but this is one job I have to do myself. It is only fair on the woman that she hears it from me.'

Richard looked at Mary and realised that Thomas must have told her about Simone. He stood up.

'Right then, we must be off if we're to catch the Belfast train.'

Thomas hugged Mary and told her he would be back in four days. Then he walked to end of the driveway with Richard.

There were four other people in the coach, so it was a tight squeeze for the two of them to get in.

The new train to Belfast was the easier part of the journey. Thomas and Richard were amazed at the scenery that the line had cut through, even if the journey took over three hours.

'Did you tell Mary about how little time you will be at home if you're elected to Parliament?' Richard asked, as they got settled into their carriage.

'Not yet, as I may not get elected.'

'From what I hear from John it seems that you have a very good chance.'

Thomas sensed that Richard wasn't happy at him meeting with the woman who looked so much like his deceased wife.

'Richard, listen to me. I think I know what you're thinking. 'Listen', he said firmly, 'I am very happily married to Mary and my life is at home with her and my family. Why on earth would I risk that for a woman who happens to look like my late wife?'

'That's the problem, Thomas. She's not just like her in looks but it's like having Christina come alive again.

'Relax, my friend. You have absolutely nothing to worry about. Anyway, I'll only be at your house for one day,' Thomas laughed.

'About your house, Thomas, I wanted to talk to you about that.' He paused, and looked out the train window. 'Ann and I talked about going back to Ireland to the house you built for us. We felt more at home there and there was so much for us to do and see. If I could find an honest estate manager this time then I thought that if I were to go back there a few times a year it might work out.'

'I pay you to run the estate, and if you come to Ireland what would you live on'? Thomas enquired.

'I could set up and run the button factory that John mentioned to me.'

Thomas got up and stretched himself. 'This is a long journey,' he sighed. 'It seems that everyone is trying to run my life for me these days when all I want is to get in my boat and sail off into the sunset.'

'Then what has possessed you to become an MP? It's the last job I ever expected you to do.'

'Why?' Thomas turned quickly and looked at him.

'Why? I'll tell you why, Thomas. When you set foot in Parliament you're bound to be in trouble. Big trouble. You always can see a better way of doing things and you could find yourself in deep water. If they don't throw you out within a month I'll be very surprised. You always want things done today, while in Parliament it takes them years to agree on anything,' he said, critically.

'Maybe they need someone to shake them up, Richard,' Thomas smiled, as he sat down again.

'You're from Ireland. That's enough to shake them up, and they'll just see you as trouble, anyway, as soon as you walk through the door,' he grinned.

The conversation ended as the guard walked passed shouting, 'Ten minutes to Belfast!'

When Michael found out his da was away to England, he took the horse to his meeting in Moville.

This was the third one he had attended, and he was making good friends with another young boy called Dermot. They had sat at the back of the meeting chatting as, very often, they were bored with the leader going on about Irish politics. The meeting was about to start when Michael went in and sat beside Dermot, giving him a wink. Kieran stood up and went to lock the door. 'We have some important things to discuss tonight, gentlemen, and it's very important that what you hear stays in this room.' He looked at Dermot and Michael. 'Is that clear everyone?' he asked, in a threatening tone. The two boys nodded. Kieran walked to the front and pulled down a large piece of paper that was attached to a board.

'While most of our work in the future will be protests at government departments, we can not rule out that, in the event of being confronted, we may have to resort to force to defend our protests. Now I hope it will never come to this. However, I believe that we need to be well prepared for such an event. To this end, therefore, we must all follow our National Commander's orders and arm ourselves. He paused and looked around the room, examining each face carefully, trying to gauge their reactions.

'I have a plan that will only work if everyone in this room agrees to it - and can keep it secret.'

There was murmuring among the men, and Michael looked at Dermot, who just shrugged his shoulders. 'The only place that we can get guns is in the police station.'

'Are you seriously going to attack a police station with that many armed policemen?' one of the men shouted out.

'Not attack, gentlemen, just borrow,' Kieran laughed. 'I will tell you my plan next week if you all agree. I want you all to go home now and think about what I have just said as, once we commit to using arms, then it's likely to be for a long time and may even cost some of you your lives. I'm not prepared to go forward on this unless I have one hundred per cent agreement from everyone in the room, including you two young eejits at the back,' he said, half jokingly.

There was more murmuring from everyone until the meeting closed.

As Michael and Dermot walked down the path towards the horse, Michael turned to Dermot, 'So what do you make of all that then?'

'Sounds a bit crazy to me. Michael but let's see what his plan is next week. To be honest, I didn't really join up to fight for anything - at least not like that!'

'Me neither, Michael grinned. 'Anyway, see you next week.'

Mary was baking her scone bread when John and Martha arrived to see her. It was a Saturday so Colleen and Michael were still in bed at eleven o'clock.

'How nice to see you both,' Mary smiled. 'You always seem to be on time for my scone bread, John.'

'We smelled it two miles away and couldn't resist any longer.' John laughed as he sat his daughter on his knee.

'How are you, Martha?' Mary asked, as she took the baby from her arms and held him up.

'Look at the size of my nephew! Martha, you must be feeding him with good food,' Martha nodded.

'I'm hoping the hot weather will come back. It was strange to have it in April. I hope that wasn't our summer,' Martha replied. 'Where's Thomas?'

'He had to go to England again with Richard to sort out some important business, but he'll be back on Tuesday.' Mary got them all to sit down while she made tea to have with her freshly-made scone bread and jam.

'If Thomas becomes an MP, Mary, how will you live without him?' Martha asked.

'What do you mean? He'll still be around, won't he?'

'Not from what I hear. He'll be away for four months at a time.'

John tried to get Martha's attention as he wanted to let Thomas break this news, not Martha. She knew John was helping Thomas get elected and it had become a point of contention between them.

'Are you sure, Martha? Who told you that?' Mary sounded very concerned.

'I'm sure Thomas will be home plenty - with all the new trains and boats we have now. London's not as far away as it used to be,' John interjected.

'He'll have to live in London from September to Christmas and January to June,' Martha retorted. 'Doesn't sound like a family job to me.'

Mary poured the tea, but seemed upset. 'I'm sure God would not take him away to work in London without thinking about us back home.'

John was making faces at Martha, which she was deliberately ignoring. 'Maybe it's not God who is taking him away,' she said. 'I've heard it might be someone else.'

'I think it's time we left Mary in peace now, Martha, and let the children play on the beach,' John said, standing up.

'You haven't started your tea yet, John. Sit down and rest yourself,' Mary said, with tears in her eyes.

Thomas and Richard's train stopped at their local station and the two jumped down onto the platform. 'This is the very place our adventure started Richard,' Thomas said sadly. 'This is where Lord Shrewsbury's pompous driver met us twenty three years ago and took us to our dream world.'

Richard patted Thomas on his back. 'Those were great days, all right, but look where they led us.'

'I hope your driver will meet us, Richard. I'm getting too old for this travelling.' Thomas walked ahead to the station gate.

It was dinner time when they arrived at the house and Ann and Simone were sitting having a glass of sherry in the living room when Thomas and Richard opened the door.

'Evening ladies,' Thomas said, as he went to the drinks cabinet. 'I hope there's a big dinner waiting. We haven't eaten since breakfast.'

Ann and Simone turned around.

'I wasn't expecting to see you, Thomas,' Ann started, as she stood up and gave him a hug. 'What brings you back this time?.'

'I'll tell you later, Ann. I'll only be here for a day.'

Dinner was quiet that evening as they were tired after their long journey. They all retired to bed early. Thomas grabbed Richard by the arm as they were going out the dining room door. 'Can you get me a trap for the morning, please.'

'Why? Richard answered, surprised.

'A wee trip planned, my friend,' Thomas smiled patting him on the shoulder. 'All will be well.'

Richard sighed and shook his head. 'Away to bed with you, my mad Irish friend.'

The next morning the rain had stopped and the sun appeared as they all came down for breakfast.

'Simone,' Thomas said as he sat down. 'I would like to take you for a short trip today.'

Simone looked shyly at everyone else. 'Just me, Thomas?.

'Yes. I would like to show you some things that the others have already seen. So yes, just you.'

Simone started eating her eggs and blushed as she knew the others would be looking at her.

'Ann. I hear that you and Richard would like to come back to your house in Ireland,' Thomas said, as he started his scrambled eggs.

Ann nearly choked on her toast. 'Goodness I didn't know Richard would tell you so soon, Thomas. It was just an idea which we were going to discuss with you some day.'

'I think it's a great idea as Richard could run my new project in Derry,' Thomas laughed at Richard who was trying not to show his emotions. 'The big problem, of course, would be who we would get to run the this estate, as we couldn't afford to have another gangster like the last one.'

Richard was very quiet and picked up a newspaper. Simone looked surprised, and asked 'What happened with the last person?'

'Richard found him, Simone, and thought he was a good man. At first he seemed to be everything he told us he was and Richard thought he could be left alone. It was only after nearly two years that our bank account was running low on funds that we found out the man had been stealing our money. When Richard returned we found the he had sold five hundred acres of my estate and left this house in a terrible state. It has taken Richard and Ann nearly two years to bring it back to its original glory.'

'That's shocking. Did you have him arrested?' Simone asked, very concerned.

'No. I believe he will find his reward someday. I am not a man of revenge.'

'I told you he had a big heart, Simone.' Richard shook his head. 'If the man had sold the entire estate Thomas would still have forgiven him.'

'It is just as well God runs this world, Richard, not us,' Thomas laughed, as he finished his breakfast.

'Now Simone let's go for our wee trip.'

Mary went upstairs and shouted down the corridor. 'It's ten thirty, you two! Are you are both coming with me to mass today? Hurry up and get dressed and you might have time for breakfast.'

Colleen and Michael were both shocked at their ma as she had never got them up for mass before. Both struggled out of bed and got dressed.

Michael came down first. 'Why do you want us to go to mass today, ma? Has someone died?'

'No, son. No one has died, but it's about time we all went as there are a lot of things to pray for.'

Colleen came down in a new dress. 'That's a bit flashy for mass, Colleen,' Mary commented as she cleared away plates from the table.

'It's brand new, ma, and it's all I have. Anyway, I wasn't expecting to go to mass. What's on today?'

'Nothing special, I just don't want my children drifting away from God, especially at this time of life.'

Colleen and Michael exchanged rolling eyes as they grabbed what was left of breakfast.

The church was packed that Sunday morning and Mary had trouble finding a place for the three of them to sit. Some of Mary's friends were surprised to see her two children with her and smiled over at her. The priest spoke about the need to be more tolerant in society today as Jesus accepted people where they were at in life. He also said that, while it was good for society to change in Ireland, it was important to keep the values that Jesus talked about in the New Testament.

Mass was over within an hour and everyone streamed out into the sunshine. John came up behind Mary. 'I'm glad you and the family were able to make it today, Mary. It was a good sermon.'

'Yes it was John. It's a pity Thomas was not here to hear it too,' Mary said sadly.

'He'll be back in a few days, Mary, and we'll be starting his electioneering as soon as possible.'

'So it took my sister to tell me the truth about the amount of time Thomas will be in London.'

John was embarrassed, and looked down. 'I'm sure Thomas was about to tell you. Maybe he didn't want to upset you.'

Mary turned to John. 'Forgive me, John, if I don't seem enthusiastic about him being elected as our next MP. It's just the first time he went England he was away for three years. He married an English girl, and only that she died, he would still be there. He came home out of guilt and was surprised that you had rescued me from America. So you see, that's why I don't intend to become an absent wife. What if he falls for his late wife's sister?' she asked, anxiously.

John was speechless and seemed upset. 'May I offer the three of you a lift in my carriage as Martha didn't come this morning.'

There was silence all the way home with Mary finding it hard to hide the tears in her eyes.

John dropped them at the end of their driveway as Mary said she wanted to walk for a bit. As they walked away, John called Michael back.

'I hope you took my advice, son, to stay away from that group in Moville.'

Michael shrugged his shoulders.

'If you call over to my house later we'll launch the new boat,' John said smiling.

Michael turned and walked away. 'I'll be there,' he shouted back, as he caught up with his ma.

Chapter 10

Thomas helped Simone up onto the seat of the trap. It was being pulled by one very large, brown horse. Richard stood at the front door watching and seemed sad watching them head off down the long driveway.

'Where are we going, sir?' Simone asked, nervously.

'A little surprise, Simone. I have two places I think you'll find interesting, and they're not far away.'

Thomas turned right onto the main track that went to the railway station. After half a mile he turned left onto a smaller narrow track and slowed down, as the track was not often used.

Twenty minutes later the track went into a wood, with a lake on the right side. A few minutes down the track, Thomas brought the trap to a stop and climbed down. He went around to the far side and held out his hand for Simone to join him. He walked her to the edge of the lake and then turned to face her. 'This is where your father died twenty years ago.' He turned and looked sadly down at the lake.

'What happened, Thomas?' She asked sadly. 'How did my daddy die?'

'It was never easy for the police to work out precisely, but it would appear that the coach may have swerved to avoid hitting a deer, hit a stone and overturned. The coach then rolled down the slope and ended up in the lake. Richard came along shortly afterwards and raced down to pull your father out of the coach, that was filling with water. Sadly, he died in Richard's arms, as he must have hit his head on the carriage roof.'

'That's awful. My poor father! I hope he didn't suffer too much.'

'He went very quickly' Thomas said 'The poor driver was also killed instantly.'

Simone looked like she wanted to cry.

'Let me take you to a happier place now,' he said, leading her back up the slope to the trap.

Twenty minutes later they arrived at the lake, which was one of the most scenic places in the county. The lake that Thomas and Richard had created was now surrounded by trees and bushes. Today the water was dark blue and the sun was reflected on the still water.

'This was once a valley, Simone. One day, while we were out doing the survey for our maps I suddenly had a vision of what this might look like as it is today. We brought your father here and suggested to him that the valley be flooded with a dam at the far end to generate electricity. He thought about it for a few minutes as he gazed in that direction. Eventually, he turned to us and agreed to do it. It cost him a lot of money at the start, but eventually he was able to persuade The Municipality that it would benefit the community. Now it's the biggest source of income for the estate as it provides electricity and drinking water for all the towns within twenty miles.'

'How amazing, Thomas! You are a very clever man,' Simone smiled.

Thomas paused, then led her down to the water's edge.

'I have another reason to bring you here, Simone.' Thomas took a deep breath. 'What I am about to tell you now may come as a great shock to you.' He paused, and could feel his stomach tightening. Simone stared at him with a concerned look on her face.

'Simone.' He paused, nervously. 'You are not Simone.' He stopped and waited for a reaction, which didn't come. She just looked into his face blankly.

'Simone, your real name is Caroline. Lady Caroline Shrewsbury - after your real mother. Your real mother, Caroline, is not a French lady called Renee.'

Simone turned pale and looked as if she was going to faint. Thomas tightened his grip on her hands. Her eyes began to fill up, and she mumbled ' What do you mean?

'When Lady Shrewsbury was in labour in the house, there was a doctor and nurse present as well as some of the staff. When the baby was delivered it was Christina, my late wife. After a few minutes the doctor suddenly announced that there was a second baby. That was you. When you were delivered, there was a problem, as you were blue and wouldn't cry. They thought you were dead, but the doctor kept smacking your back until you started to cry, and eventually you opened your eyes. However, at that stage, your mother screamed that she didn't want a second baby and to take you away. I think she thought there was something wrong with you. The doctor and Lord Shrewsbury tried to calm her down and reason with her.

However, that initial experience meant that she never bonded with you, her second baby, and this rejection continued for a month. Eventually your father agreed to have you adopted. Your mother had developed what people thought was a mental condition. It was only when she died that they discovered that she had a brain tumour. Your father was about to give you up for adoption when your nanny, Renee, offered to raise you as her own child. Even though she was not able to raise you herself, she still couldn't bear to see you be adopted by a stranger. Your father eventually agreed and bought her a large house in the country outside Manchester and gave her an income for life. So that was when Renee brought you up as her own.

We employed a rogue estate manager four years ago and we didn't know that he had cut off Renee's money. That is why her financial circumstances changed.'

Simone was crying openly now, and Thomas took her in his arms and let her cry for on his shoulder.

He pulled away and took her face in his hands. 'It doesn't matter who your real parents are, Simone. What matters is that you are still Simone or Caroline - or whatever you want to be called.'

'Renee will always be my mother, Thomas' She sobbed. 'She brought me up and was just the most loving mother anyone could ask for.'

'You are right, Simone. Renee brought you up as her own, while your biological mother gave you away. If I was in your position, I wouldn't find it difficult to decide who my real mother was.'

'Why do I have to find this out now? It seems to cruel,' Simone sobbed.

'I think you should take this revelation as an open door for the future and not a sad door of the past.'

Thomas said kindly. 'I believe that's what your father would have wanted. He never got over losing you and often went to see you.'

'He never did, Thomas. He never once came to see me or make himself known to me.'

'No Simone. Your father used to visit you twice a year. He would stand outside your house or school and watch you from afar. He told his staff he was going to London on business, but he was really going to see you in Manchester.' Simone was astounded!

'Why did he not come and speak to me then?'

'He told Andrew the butler that he didn't want you to find out the truth about your mother and that he was just happy to see you grow into the beautiful woman that you are today.'

Simone cried like her heart was breaking. 'Who am I Thomas? Why has this happened to me? Why would God let this happen to me?'

'He must have a very special purpose for you. A very special purpose,' he said tenderly.

Simone wiped her face with a handkerchief that Thomas gave her. 'I will never forget this day.'

Thomas took led her back to the trap. 'So ... do I call you Caroline, or Simone?'

'I will always be Simone,' she said quietly. 'I don't know who Caroline is.'

'We have a lot of practical things to sort out then, Simone, before I leave tomorrow, so I think we need to get back home. I don't drink any more, but I think I could do with a stiff brandy now,' he said, attempting to lighten the atmosphere.

Michael walked over to John's house as he wanted to do some thinking. He was convinced that the group called The Fenians were genuine in their endeavours to bring about change in Ireland. However, he wasn't so convinced of the methods they might employ to do so. When he joined, the group said they were an all-Ireland movement that would be involved in protests at government departments and organise rallies. What the leader proposed at the last meeting, however, was that they might have to defend themselves with arms at some point if they were pressurised by forces of the crown. That wasn't exactly what Michael joined up for. Now he was being forced to vote one way or other. His friend Dermot had the same concerns as they both wanted good jobs and were afraid that being with this group could ruin their life chances - in the event of things going wrong. He would need to think carefully about this.

Michael walked round to the back of the house where he found John stripping off to his vest and looking very hot and flustered.

'Did you figure out how to get the boat to the sea John?' Michael asked as he ran his hand over the new paint work on the bow of the boat.

'Look,' replied John, smiling and pointing to a row of rollers behind the boat. 'Cut all those myself while you were spending your days sleeping.'

'That's very clever.' Michael could see that the rollers stretched all the way to the sea. 'You must have cut down all my da's trees to make that amount,'

'There are a few left, but you're going to have to help me with the first push.'

John came around and stood beside Michael. 'Once the boat starts moving it'll roll nicely to the water. To get it to the slope we'll have to use the two horses. Now the problem is that once the boat starts to move on its own we will only have a few seconds to disconnect the ropes from the horses or the weight of the thing will pull them both into the sea.'

Michael could see this was a very dangerous operation. 'The idea is that the ropes will not actually be tied to the boat but spun around these hooks. We'll have to try and hold them so they don't pull loose. As soon as the boat is on the slope we'll let go of the ropes and grab the bow lines that are hanging down. If we miss those then the boat will head on down the river with us chasing after it like mad eejits,' he laughed. Michael was not convinced, but had to give it a try.

'Are you ready then?' John shouted. 'Give the horses a shout.'

Michael whacked the rains and shouted at the horses and they started to pull. The boat groaned as the horses tried hard to pull against the heavy boat. After a few seconds of Michael shouting at them it started to move. 'Good, lad. Don't let your rope go now!' The boat started to move quite freely and was soon on the rollers. Suddenly it took off and Michael and John dropped the ropes. The horses jumped out of the way. It started to slide down the rollers much faster that John had anticipated and they were now both running after it on each side.

'I can't reach the bow rope!' Michael shouted. He couldn't hear what John shouted in return and within a few seconds the boat was going so fast that they couldn't keep up with it. It hurtled down the ramp and went into the sea with a huge splash that sent a large wave over the small pier. Michael caught up with John and they both stood staring with disbelief.

'Right, Michael. 'Quick! The current hasn't caught it yet! You go along the pier. I'm going to swim to the boat.' John plunged into the sea and started swimming towards the boat. Michael ran along the pier to catch up with him.

John reached one of the bow ropes hanging down and started to swim to the pier, trying to pull the boat behind him. Michael was amazed how strong he was and, after five minutes, was able to reach down and grab the line, as John, exhausted, climbed out of the water.

'Phew! That was a close one!' He laughed. 'Pull her in tight, lad.'

They soon had the boat secured to the pier. 'Imagine what my da would have said if we had to call for rescue, John!'

'He will never know now, will he?' John winked. 'Let's see if we can get the steam engine started and we could sail round to your house.'

Mary and Colleen were sitting on the summer bench overlooking their pier. They were chatting about Colleen's new friend, David.

'Do you like him. Ma?' asked Colleen, as she supped her tea from her favourite mug.

'He seems a very nice young gentleman, Colleen, but I hear he's also a very powerful man in the city.'

'It's his da who has the power and money, Ma. It seems he's training his son to take that over. At present David is just the same as me in that he's learning his trade.'

'What's more important is how much you like him, Colleen.'

'I like him very much, Ma. I'll be very careful about who I start a relationship with as I still believe God wants me to have the right person.'

'I'm pleased to hear that, because I was worried that you had lost your faith.'

'I doubted for a while, Ma, but you brought me up to be a thinker, so I did a lot of thinking and realised, in the end, that most of what you taught me made a lot of sense.'

Mary was about to speak again when they both heard a boat coming round the corner. It was heading to their pier.

'Who's that?' Colleen stood up and gazed out to sea.

The boat slowed down and, a few minutes later, pulled up at the far side of the pier.

'That's some size of boat, Colleen,' Mary said, as she walked towards the pier.

The boat stopped, and John and Michael jumped out.

'Well look at you two!' Mary shouted. 'Where on earth did you get a boat like that?'

'Michael and I made it, Mary,' John stated, proudly. 'It's taken us a year, but it's finished now.'

Mary and Colleen went over to look at it. 'This is a real fine piece of work,' Mary exclaimed. 'I can't believe the two of ye made this!'

'Now you see where Michael has been this last year - when you thought he was away dreaming,' John said, with satisfaction, patting Michael on the back.

'I'm very proud of you, Son, and my apologies for giving you a hard time.

Michael went over and his ma gave him a hug. 'Thanks, Ma. It was really John who designed it, and we built it for Da.'

'Well, Son. let's pray that he decides to take up fishing instead of going to London.'

Michael said nothing and smiled at Colleen.

Thomas was up early for breakfast the next morning as he wanted to catch the nine o'clock train. Richard came down and stood beside him as he was gazing out the dining room window at the fountains.

'All is well then, Thomas?' Richard asked, apprehensively.

'Yes. I told Simone. She was very upset at first, but has taken it well. Now I just need to get home. I have a great wife and family and I need to get back to them straight away.'

'Yes, but if you get elected to parliament will you be spending more time here?' Richard enquired. 'You'll have to get used to leaving them then.'

Thomas turned to him and smiled. 'You're always looking out for me Richard. You are the greatest friend I could ever have, and I'll always listen to what you say. Please don't worry. I haven't made a final decision yet about standing for parliament, even though I told John I would. Pray for me that I make the right decision. Now ... about Simone,' Thomas moved away from the window and poured himself a cup of tea, ' ... I've been thinking.'

'Oh dear,' Richard replied, smiling. 'That means trouble ahead.'

'If you and Ann would seriously like to move back to Ireland then why don't I sell the estate and give part of the money to Simone?'

Richard nearly choked on the toast he was eating. 'Are you serious Thomas?' he exclaimed.

'It's just an idea, Richard. The sale of it would give us a huge amount of money to live forever in Ireland. It would mean Simone could start her own life wherever she wanted. This estate is going to become very hard to run in years to come, and why should we give ourselves so much worry?'

Richard was quiet for a few moments.

'Did you not promise Sir Henry that the estate would never be sold?' he asked.

'I did, but it would be of great benefit to his niece.' Thomas grabbed his bag.

'Think about it, Richard,' he shouted, as he hurried out the door.

Chapter 11

Michael arranged to meet Dermot down by the pier in Moville. He sat staring out at the River Foyle as one of the fishing boats was coming in.

'Penny for your thoughts, Michael,' Dermot said, as he came up behind him.

'You would need more than a penny for my thoughts, Dermot. You couldn't afford them,' he laughed.

'What way are ye going to vote tonight?' Dermot asked, sitting down beside him.

'I was thinking of leaving the group. It's not going the way I thought. If we both vote against action they might give us trouble,' Michael replied with a serious tone.

'I know Kieran and his family. I don't think he would do that. He seems a reasonable sort of a fella.'

'Will we go and see then how it plays out?' Michael looked at Dermot and could see he had fear in his eyes.

Kieran locked the door of the meeting room again once all twenty men were inside. He checked all around the windows and door to make sure they were secure and that no one was listening.

'Right men,' he started. 'We'll start with the vote. Let me quite clear again. We take no action unless there's a full vote here tonight. If anyone votes against we will not take any action against that person, but we'd expect you to leave the group.'

He walked up and down the front of the room rubbing his hands together. 'All those in favour of taking action to protect our protests, please raise your hand now.'

Every man in the room raised their hand except Michael and Dermot. Kieran and the others in the room turned and stared at them. Eventually Kieran walked down the back and stood looking down at them. 'So, lads, were you clear about what you were supposed to do? You don't want to vote, right? Is that correct? I'd like to know why.'

Michael looked at Dermot, then timidly answered. 'We don't want to get involved with something that would get us into trouble, sir.'

'By coming here, lads, you are already in trouble.' Kieran gave a false smile. 'It would be hard for you to leave safely now as you've heard a bit too much.'

'We just want to leave and go home now,' Dermot said, nervously.

'Well you can't lads. I'm sorry, because we need you to do a wee job first. If you do this well, then you can home.' He pulled a chair around to face them. 'You see, we've a job planned tonight. As you are the only two people in this room that know nothing about the details, it means we have total secrecy.'

'Our parents will be looking for us if we don't go home soon,' Michael chipped in, scared.

'You'll be home in an hour son, and then you'll never hear from us again.' Kieran gave a smirk.

He turned and spoke to the rest of the men. 'Right men off you go.' The men filed out of the room and then there was silence.

'The men are going to Greencastle to start a big rumpus in Doherty's pub,' Kieran said, smiling.

'In half an hour all the police will be called out to break up the disturbance. That's where you lads come in. All you have to do is stroll into the police station - which will be empty. When you enter, take the door on your right and over on the far wall will be a cabinet full of rifles and handguns. The cabinet is locked but you'll find the key in the top drawer of the big table. You simply open the cabinet and help yourself to as many weapons as you can carry. Bring them down to a farm cart that's parked outside the station. Pull the cover back and hide the guns in the hay. When you've done that, just walk down the street chatting away as if you were out for as stroll. When you reach the town square just head home as if you had enjoyed a night out with your friend. Then go straight home.'

'What if there's a policeman still in the station?' Dermot asked, shaking.

'There'll be no police in the station. They'll be away at the big fight. If anyone comes along just pretend you're going in to report a stolen cow.'

'We can't do that, Kieran, as we'll get the blame for everything if we're caught' Dermot said.

Kieran looked at them with a threatening face. 'You have no choice, lads, if you ever want to see your families again.'

He stood up and marched them to the door. 'Wait till we see the police all run to the police carriage, and then you stroll casually up the street. It'll be dark in ten minutes, so no one will see you.'

Michael and Dermot looked at each other with fear in their eyes, but said nothing.

'Off you go, lads. Good luck.'

Ten minutes after the sun had gone down, Dermot and Michael heard a commotion and saw four policemen race out of the station and jump into the police carriage. Michael recognised one of them as Sergeant O'Hare. He was sick in his stomach, but knew he had to obey Kieran.

They started walking casually up the street towards the police station. 'Stay calm, Dermot, and it'll be all right. We're only going to borrow a few guns,' Michael said, as he led the way.

When they got there, they couldn't believe that the police had left the front door unlocked. Michael called in the door. 'Anyone there?'

There was no answer so they knew it was safe to go on in. The door on the right was open and Michael went straight to the big table and opened the drawer. There was a bunch of keys - and not just one, as they had been told. He quickly ran to the gun cupboard. His hands were shaking as he tried key after key but not one would open the door. 'What do we do now?' Michael asked, in desperation.

'Try that big one, Michael.' Dermot breathed, frantically.

The big key worked and the door swung open. Michael handed Dermot two rifles, which he immediately dropped on the ground.

'These are very heavy,' he whimpered.

'Two each will do then,' Michael said, quietly. 'Here ... stuff a few handguns into your belt and let's get out of here.'

Michael grabbed three rifles and they ran for the exit. He looked back to make sure no one was following them and followed Dermot out the front door.

They had only gone a few paces when suddenly guns started firing at them from the road. Dermot dropped to the ground. Michael felt a terrible pain in his chest and slumped over Dermot's body laying there. Then there was black.

Thomas was finishing a nice Irish stew that Mary had made to welcome him home from England.

He was in the process of telling Mary his plans to sell the estate when they heard two horses come to a stop at their front door.

'I'll go, Thomas,' Mary said. 'Sit and rest yourself.'

A few moments later Mary showed Sergeant O'Hare and another policeman into their kitchen.

'Sergeant, good to see you,' Thomas said, as he jumped up from his seat. 'What brings you out at this time of night?'

'Can both of you take a seat, please,' O'Hare started, in a serious tone.

'There was a serious incident in Moville tonight - and Michael was involved.'

Thomas jumped up. 'What kind of incident?'

'Please, Thomas. I need you take a seat.' O'Hare and the other policeman looked at each other.

'We had a tip off that The Fenians were going to raid our police station tonight. It was a clever plan. However, they didn't know that one of their men had told us the whole plan. They set up a pretend fight in a Greencastle pub so as to draw my men away. They then forced two young men to go into our station to steal whatever arms they could get. When the two men came out it was dark, and one of my men who was hiding behind the wall thought they were aiming a rifle at him so he let off two shots and hit the robbers.' O'Hare paused and looked down at the floor. 'One of the men we shot was your son, Michael.'

'Oh, dear God, no!' Mary yelled. Thomas just stared at O'Hare.

'Is he dead?' Thomas asked, fearfully.

'No, but he's badly injured. He's in the hospital in Derry. The other young man was not so fortunate.'

Thomas and Mary fell into each other's arms and cried openly.

'We arrested the whole group. The informant told that me that

Michael and his friend Dermot didn't want to have anything to do with the plan. They were forced into it by Kieran, their leader.'

'We must go to him straight away, Sergeant,' Mary said, grabbing her coat and hat.

'Not a good idea, folks. I'm sorry. They won't let you in to see him till he regains consciousness. The bullet only hit his shoulder but when he fell back he banged his head. The doctor said that in time he should come round.'

'Thank you, Alfred, for letting us know. We appreciate you coming to tell us,' Thomas said.

The two policemen went to leave but O'Hare turned back. 'When Michael recovers, hopefully there will be no charges against him. He was clearly set up. We'll be charging the others, though, and they'll spend a long time in jail.'

Thomas and Mary sat stunned, holding each others hands, as the policemen left.

Twenty minutes later, Colleen came bouncing in from meeting with her friend. She quickly realised something was wrong and was shocked when her parents told her what happened.

The next morning all three of them were up early as Thomas planned to take his coach to visit Michael. As they were going out the front door, Thomas noticed a new boat in his harbour.

'Where did that come from, Mary?' he asked, as they walked towards the coach.

'John and Michael made it for you, Thomas,' Mary answered sadly.

Thomas broke away from them and almost ran to the pier. He rubbed his hand across the bow of the new boat, with tears in his eyes. 'Dear God, let him live,' he prayed, as he looked at the boat with sadness and amazement.

'Can we stop at my office to let them know I won't be in work today?' Colleen asked, as Thomas climbed into the coach behind them.

'Yes, of course. It's only a short distance from your office to the new hospital at the top of Clarendon Street.' Thomas closed the door and shouted to the driver to leave.

The white building was one long two-storey construction with a small t-section at the far end. When they went in the front door, a nurse told them to walk down a long corridor till they came to a door on the right. The room was long and narrow with rows of beds on each side. A nurses' room at the bottom had a glass window that overlooked the ward. Every bed was made up with a red blanket and a white pillow. There were only two patients in the room, and they could see Michael at the far end. A nurse came over to greet them.

'We are Michael Sweeney's family,' Thomas said. 'Can we see him yet?'

'Michael regained consciousness this morning and he can now speak,' the nurse started.' If you can wait here please, I'll ask the doctor to speak to you.'

The nurse walked to a room at the other end of the ward and she was escorted back by a man in a white coat.

'Mr. Sweeney,' the doctor said, as he shook Thomas's hand and acknowledged Mary and Colleen with a slight bow. 'Your son has had a very lucky escape. The bullet went right through his shoulder and has torn a muscle. It also cracked his shoulder blade. It'll take some time to heal and he'll be very sore for quite some time. The bang on the head from falling to the ground has caused some concussion but again, with rest, he should recover. If the bullet had been four inches lower it would have killed him instantly by passing through his heart, so I would say that someone was looking after him.'

'Thank you so much for all that you have done. We all deeply appreciate it.'

The doctor turned to Mary and Colleen. 'Your son will need to rest here for a week but then should make a full recovery. I think he would be glad to see you.' He then pointed to in the direction of the ward and walked away.

'Well, Son,' Thomas smiled, as he sat on Michael's bed.

'I'm so sorry, Da. It was so stupid of me.'

'Not a word, Michael.' Thomas stroked his son's hair out of his eyes. 'Sergeant O'Hare has told us the whole story and there's no blame attached to you or Dermot. You had no choice in what you did.' Michael looked perplexed, but greatly relieved

'How's Dermot, Da?'

Thomas took a deep breath and sat closer to his son. 'He wasn't as lucky as you, Michael. I'm afraid he died instantly.'

Michael sat transfixed for a minute and then, as the realization that his friend was gone began to sink in, he began to cry. 'We both wanted to leave, Da,' he sobbed. 'Dermot was scared and wanted to run home, but the man threatened us saying we would never see our families again unless we did what he ordered.'

'I know, Michael. Sergeant O'Hare had an informant in the group and they knew what was going to happen. They intended just to arrest you both as you came out of the station, but one of the young policemen who was hiding behind the wall thought that Dermot was aiming a rifle at him.'

'Dermot would not have even known how to fire a rifle, Da. He was just holding two in his arms and he kept dropping them.'

'It's really sad, Michael, but it was very dark and the policeman thought he was defending himself.'

'He was my best friend, Da. He wouldn't have hurt a fly.' Michael cried. 'It's just not fair.'

Mary came round and sat on the other side of the bed. 'There'll be time to work everything out in the future, Michael. You have to get better now and we thank God that you will be coming home in a week's time.' Mary pulled the blankets up over his arms. 'Time to rest now, Son. Don't worry.'

'Dermot's ma and pa won't be saying that, Ma. I need to go and talk to them.'

'We'll see them later, Michael. We'll tell them that you'll call with them when you get better.'

Michael sank his head into the pillow, still sobbing bitterly. Thomas motioned to Mary and Colleen that it was time to leave.

As they left to get into their coach, Colleen said quietly, 'I'll walk down the street to my work. I need to do something to take my mind off what has just happened.' She walked off without saying goodbye.

Thomas and Mary started the long journey back to Greencastle. They never spoke till they were entering the driveway, when Thomas turned to Mary and said sadly, 'I won't be standing as an MP, Mary.' Mary looked into his eyes and didn't reply. She just reached over and took his hand in hers and held it tightly.

Chapter 12

John, Martha and the two children arrived at Thomas and Mary's house for lunch. John was nervous going in as he didn't know what to say to them. Martha was her usual cheerful self and smiled as if she didn't have a care in the world.

'So he's still alive!' she said, happily, as she dropped her daughter onto the soft sofa. 'It's very unlike any of our family to get into bother, now, isn't it?'

Thomas and Mary, who were sitting were very depressed, took some time to reply.

'It's hard to kill a Sweeney now isn't it, Thomas?'

Thomas smiled for the first time in two days.

'It's harder to keep you quiet, Martha,' he said, shaking his head, 'especially when something goes wrong.'

'It was my ma who taught me to rejoice in God for all things, so you can blame her.'

John looked a bit embarrassed. 'I'm sure that's not what Thomas and Mary need to hear right now, Martha,' he said, trying to stop his girls from fighting over their seat.

'Actually, for once my sister is right, John. We're sitting here full of self-pity when we should be thanking God our son's still alive.' Mary went to the stove to put the kettle on.

'How is he, anyway?' John asked, trying to take control of the situation.

'He is doing fine, John, and will be home next Monday,' Thomas said, quietly.

'I tried to warn him many times about getting involved with that group, but he wouldn't listen.'

'Where would he get that stubbornness from, now?' Martha laughed, winking at her brother-in-law.

Thomas grinned, but then changed the subject. 'That's a mighty fine boat that you and Michael built for me.'

'Michael did most of the work. All I did was design it and show him step by step what to do. You should be very proud of him.'

'Oh I am, John. Thank you for taking the time to work with him. I'm sure it'll pay off once he comes home.' Thomas went to the stove and poured himself a cup of coffee. 'We started drinking this in America. Have you tried it yet?' John just shrugged his shoulders. There was an awkward silence between them all as the reality of the situation sank in. Thomas broke it by saying sadly. 'His group were only intending to do what The Liberal Party wants to do. That is, bring about self government for our wee land. Their means of achieving it were wrong, but they had the right idea. By the way, I won't be standing as an MP now, John, even though I believe in their policies. No local person would vote for me now knowing that my son had joined The Fenians.'

John was silent, but eventually said. 'I understand, Thomas. I'll let them know today.'

Colleen was working in her office when William came in the door. 'Colleen, we have a new case coming in next week from one of our top clients,' he stated, as he threw a bundle of notes on her desk. 'I'm well aware that you have never dealt with a divorce case before, but this is a good one to start on as the gentleman concerned is very pleasant and he seems to be able to communicate better with females.'

'Who is he, sir?' Colleen asked, suspecting that she was being dropped into another so-called learning situation.

'The name is in there, with all the details. The wife is a lovely lady, and they have four daughters. They've threatened to divorce on two occasions before. Perhaps it will happen this time around so that we can get paid!' William smiled, and went into his own office.

Colleen sneaked out quietly to Elaine in reception. 'Do you know a Simon Watters?' She asked quietly.

'Oh no! Is he back again?' Elaine exclaimed.

'William wants me to handle his divorce, and I think he's secretly hoping it actually goes through this time.'

'The last two times he got to the day of the court and then pulled out.' Elaine got out of her chair and came around beside Colleen. 'Let me have a quick glance at the papers.'

'Better not let William see us laughing about this,' she giggled.

Elaine had a quick look through the papers and then sat back down. 'Yes that's the man. Only this time he looks like he's serious. He didn't have lists of his assets before, so he must be expecting this to go ahead.'

'I suppose he's very wealthy,' Colleen sighed.

'All our clients are very wealthy, Colleen. This man owns a huge yacht on the river. It's big enough to go to America.'

Colleen headed into her office. 'Thanks, Elaine,' she called back.

Richard arrived at his front door in their best coach. Andrew, the butler came out to open the door for him. 'You shouldn't be doing this, Andrew. Where's Simon, my valet?'

'He's busy, sir, and it's always an honour to serve you,' Andrew replied.

'Listen, my man. You made a great decision in telling us about

Simone. Thomas took her away last week and told her the truth about her mother. She was very upset at first but is now like a new person - once she found out the truth. None of this would have happened if you hadn't told us. So thank you very much, Andrew.'

'I still feel bad about breaking confidence, sir. It was the hardest thing I have ever had to do.' He opened the front door for Richard to enter. 'Andrew,' Richard called, as he walked away. 'You told me that you've been working here for forty years. Is that right?'

'It is, sir. I started here as a stable boy when I was twenty and worked my way up to chief butler and housekeeper.'

'That makes you sixty,' Richard paused. 'Have you ever thought of retiring?'

'I have, sir. I've been putting money aside for a long time and, before he died, Lord Shrewsbury sold me a small house down by the river. It was so little money that I presume he was almost giving it to me. I will retire there and fish.'

Richard came up to face Andrew and looked at him kindly. 'Just supposing we were to sell this estate, would you stay on for the new owner or would you like to retire?'

'I was wondering when you might say that, sir.' He paused and looked down at the floor. 'I think I would retire as I would never find anyone like you and Thomas, sir. This house holds too many memories of wonderful people like yourselves and I would find it hard to work for anyone else.'

'Nice of you to say that, Andrew. By the way, please keep this conversation to yourself as it's only a thought between us at present and may not happen. You're the only person that Thomas and I were concerned for as this house is almost your home.'

Andrew bowed politely and walked away.

Just then Simone came walking down the stairs.

'Good day, Simone. I was wondering if I might trouble you for a moment please?'

'Certainly Richard. I was just going to the drawing room for some tea, if you'd like to join me.'

How quickly she has adjusted to her surroundings, Richard thought, as he followed her into the room.

'How do you see your future, Simone?' Richard asked, abruptly, as he sat down beside her on the sofa.

'My future is in your hands, Richard, as I hardly know what day of the week it is right now. I am now Lady Caroline Shrewsbury and live in a grand estate that I don't even own. My new house that you and Thomas have given me will be ready next week so I'll be living alone. I don't know anyone locally, and most people will know me as Simone. I can hardly change my name to Lady Simone Macron, which was my mother's family name. If I stay here I would have to become someone I'm not and live a life that, I feel, would be totally fraudulent.'

Richard was shocked with her honesty, and felt uncomfortable. 'I see, Simone. I'm very glad you told me that.'

'What would you like to do, if you were given the opportunity?'

'Lord Shrewsbury set me up with a business in Manchester. I was selling ladies' fashion clothes to the rich and famous. I enjoyed it for a while but got tired of dealing with entitled people and couldn't stand the idle gossip that went on between the women who came in every week. Please don't get me wrong. I've nothing against people with money. It's just that I prefer people like you and Ann, who seem so kind and so real.'

'We both come from working class backgrounds, miss. We're only here because of an extraordinary run of circumstances - which you'd find hard to believe. Thomas, who owns this house, and who has become one of the wealthiest men in England, comes from a very poor background in Ireland, and that's why we don't count our wealth as anything to hold on to.'

'I've come to love the three of you very much as friends and the thought of losing you at any time would make me very sad. It's hard to find genuine people today.'

'That's very kind of you to say that, Simone. That, then, makes what I'm about to say more difficult.'

Simone turned to Richard and looked alarmed.

'Thomas is seriously thinking about selling the estate and giving you a substantial part of the sale.

Ann and I would then move to a house that we own beside Thomas and Mary in Ireland. Like you, we don't really fit into this lifestyle.'

Simone looked shocked and Richard could see that her eyes were starting to water. She was quiet for a long time, staring blankly at the fire.

'We wouldn't like to see you being left on your own, Simone, and were wondering if you had any friends you could live with?'

'If Thomas was giving me money do you think I could come with you to Ireland and live nearby?' she asked, hopefully.

Richard nearly choked on his sandwich. 'Goodness, that's an idea!' He stood up and put his teacup on the table. 'That's something I would have to consult with Thomas about as he owns all the land in that part of the country.'

'Ann and I have become such close friends and she's the first real friend I've ever had. It would be hard for me to adjust to making new friends in Ireland, but a lot easier than here.'

'Listen. Let's talk again in a few days' time, Simone,' Richard said.

Thomas and Mary arrived at the hospital in their coach on Monday morning. Thomas talked to the doctor again who assured him that Michael was fine. He said he would have to keep his arm in a sling for six weeks and get plenty of rest. Mary didn't see Thomas hand the doctor a substantial cheque towards finishing the new hospital which had just been opened.

Michael looked very depressed as he said goodbye to the hospital staff. He still couldn't believe his best friend was gone. On the way home, Michael suddenly broke the silence by asking his ma, 'How was Dermot's funeral?'

'It was very sad, Michael, and his parents were totally distraught.' Mary said.

'I should have been the one to die, Ma. He was such a good lad compared to me.'

'Don't ever think like that, Michael. We're all the same in God's sight, and it is nothing to do with how good or bad we are. He was very blessed to have you as a friend.'

'We were both going to leave the group, you know, Ma, and that night we just wanted to go home. I should have persuaded him to run away.'

'You wouldn't have got far as the gang had it planned all along that you would get the guns. They didn't have the courage to do it themselves.'

Thomas looked at Michael, fondly. 'They were bad men, Michael.

Not to worry, Son. You won't be seeing any of them again for a very long time. It's time to forget now and look forward to the future.'

'What future, Da? Who would want me now?' Michael sighed.

'Everyone knows what happened, Son, and they know that you are innocent.'

'I wanted the same outcome as you, Da.'

'I know, Thomas, but there was a big difference in the way those dreams might have come to pass.'

'Will you still become an MP, Da?'

Thomas looked at Mary, then back to Michael, and answered slowly. 'No, Michael. It would seem both our plans are over for now.'

'You can't give up because of me, Da. Please go on.'

'Thank you, Michael, but I already had doubts before this incident and I've made up my mind now. I think you and I would be safer fishing. What do you think?' He laughed, and even Michael smiled.

As they approached Moville, Thomas told them he wanted to stop at the post office. He went in and sent a telegram to Richard, before coming back to the coach. He gave a big sigh as he sat down beside Mary. ' I've just told Richard to sell the estate,' he announced, smiling.

'Oh my goodness, Thomas! That's a major decision!' Mary gasped.

'Richard and Ann would like to come and live beside us in their new house, Mary. They're tired of pretending to be royalty in my big mansion and agree with me that it will become harder to keep in years to come.'

'I'm very fond of Ann. She's so easy to get on with. It would be great to have them living here again.' Mary said excitedly.

'If, and when, the estate sells, I intend to give Simone a very large portion of it. She is, after all, the only surviving blood relation of Lord Shrewsbury. It'll help her to start a new life. We owe her that.'

Mary gave Thomas a nod, before she turned to Michael. 'Your Da is thinking of opening a new factory in Derry, Son. If you're nice to him he might give you a job,' she laughed.

'What sort of factory, Da.' Michael asked, brightening up.

'Buttons.' Thomas looked out the window. 'Buttons,' he said, grinning broadly.

Chapter 13

Colleen was having a last look through the divorce papers while she was waiting for the client to come in. William came out of his office, putting his coat on. 'Colleen don't be put off by this loud character. Just make sure he signs the papers and agrees to the court date.' He went to leave her office when he turned and added, 'Make sure he knows that we charge £200 for a divorce case and expect a deposit this time as he never paid us for the last two failures.'

When he left the office, Elaine came in laughing. 'Listen Colleen, you need to know about Mr, Watters.' She glanced out the front door to make sure they were on their own. 'He's the most eccentric person I have ever met. He wears bright colour clothes that don't match and a hat that makes him look like he has just stepped out of a circus. He has a reputation of being very fond of the women, and I'd say that's why his wife wants a divorce.'

'But it's not his wife who filing for divorce Elaine! It's him.'

'Yes. I know, but he thinks if he does it first she won't get so much of his money.'

'Well, he's come to the wrong lawyer if that's what he thinks,' Colleen said, standing up.' I've been digging into his assets and can I just say that he's being economical with his truth about what he's really worth.'

'Just how much is he worth then?' Elaine asked, putting her hands on her hips.

Just then the front door opened and they heard a man's voice calling, 'Hello! I'm here.'

Elaine rushed out the door to find Mr. Watters standing in the front office holding a bunch of flowers. 'These are for you, young lady. I found them in a hedge on the way over here and thought to myself, which pretty lady can I give these to?' he said, charmingly.

'Why thank you kindly Mr. Watters. How sweet of you, but I'm sure you didn't find them in a hedge.'

'So is William waiting for me to get this nonsense over with?' he enquired, as he headed for Colleen's office.

'I'm afraid it's not William today, Mr. Watters; it's his new lawyer.' Elaine said, nervously. 'William was called to an urgent court case today and he sent his apologies. He said his new lawyer will be able to look after you just fine.'

Mr. Watters turned on his heel and walked straight into Colleen's office.

'Excuse me, Miss. Where's the lawyer?' he enquired, as he put his hat and coat on the stand.

'I'm the lawyer, sir,' Colleen replied standing up.

'You're a lawyer?' Mr. Watters shouted, looking at her disparagingly. 'Don't be so ridiculous!'

Colleen smiled and held out her hand to him. To her surprise he took it and sat down in front of her, even though he looked very uncomfortable.

'Have you won any cases?' he asked, taking a cigarette out of a gold case and lighting it with a gold lighter.

Colleen felt like running out the door but she managed to keep calm and professional.

'Yes I have Mr. Watters - quite a few recently, in fact.'

'I suppose you will have to do then, girl,' he grunted.

Colleen opened his file in front of him and was quiet for a moment, pretending to read down some of the pages.

'The first question I would like to ask you Mr. Watters is 'why?'

'Why what?'

'Why are you looking for a divorce?'

'That's a very personal question and has nothing to do with my divorce case,' he answered, coldly.

'If you want my company to represent you and get you the best terms then I must know everything about you and your reasons for divorce. Otherwise I can not win your case for you.'

Mr. Watters stared at Colleen for a moment and looked like he was about to explode. Then he sighed deeply. 'No one has ever asked me that question before.' He took a deep pull on his cigarette then stumped it out on the ashtray that Colleen had quickly provided. 'Why did you ask me that?'

Colleen took a deep breath and with a lot of courage sat straight up and drew a deep breath.

'You want to know why I asked you that, sir? Well now I'll tell you.

Firstly, I personally don't believe that divorce is always the best thing - unless in extreme circumstances. Secondly, there are no winners on either side, and sometimes it can be a very difficult process. Thirdly, in your own case, you are about to lose a huge amount of your wealth by giving your wife half your fortune. It may affect your relationship with your four daughters. I have been told that there are many men who think your wife is one of the most beautiful women in Ireland. You have to accept that, if you divorce her, she's certain to have a long queue of men wanting to marry her. They will live very comfortably off your money. Shall I continue?'

Mr. Watters just sat looking at Colleen unable to speak for a good two minutes. Colleen began to get very nervous.

'The purpose of me using your law firm is to protect my assets,' he said, firmly.

'We will protect your assets for you, when you start being honest with us, sir. If this case ever went to court, a judge would tear up your figures, as everyone in the north west knows that you are far wealthier than your figures provide. For instance, you haven't listed your ship on The Foyle which is worth a quarter of a million pounds and many of the hotels that you own in Belfast.'

'How do you know about those?' he growled.

'I do my own research into my clients as I trust no one and I don't want to be made a fool of in court.'

Mr. Watters continued to stare at Colleen and then started to laugh. 'What's your name young lady?'

'Colleen, sir,' she said sheepishly.

'Well Colleen, I wish there were more lawyers like you in this country. All the lawyers that I have used in the past have told me what they think that I want to hear from them. You are the first one to tell me the truth.'

Colleen blushed and didn't know where to look as she thought she had overstepped her position.

'What do you suggest I do then, young Colleen?'

Colleen couldn't believe his response, and was now aware that her boss might sack her for her straightforward talking.

'Well, sir. I'm too young to know about marriage relationships, but if I was in your position I would go back to my family and try and work things out with your wife. Have you two ever really been honest with each other ... talked ... really talked, together? Have you spent money on her and your four daughters? Have you tried being kind to each other? My father lost his first wife after a year of marriage and missed her dearly. You are blessed to still have such a dear person in your life, and I suspect you may regret your decision.

Mr. Watters shook his head and stood up. 'You, young lady, are quite a remarkable person, and William is very fortunate to have you here with him. I think I might just take your advice and reconsider this whole thing. I'll need to give this a lot more thought. Thank you for all the work you put in but, for now, I think I might just drop the divorce.'

'That's fine. Just one thing, Mr. Watters. If I'm to avoid being sacked by William when he comes back here, I'll have to charge you for the work that's been done so far.

Mr. Watters took out his cheque-book and laughed again. ' How much do I owe you?'

Colleen bit her lip and said quietly. 'We charge £200 for a divorce case Mr. Watters, but this is actually your third case that you owe us for.'

He sat down again and pulled out his cheque-book. As he wrote the cheque for £600, Colleen sat speechless.

'Tell the old geezer he'll owe me a dinner some night,' Mr. Watters said as he got up and walked out.

Colleen sat there with a huge smile on her face.

Elaine came running in a few moments later. 'Well how did that go?'

'Good.' Colleen seemed in a dream 'I got a big cheque off him.'

'A cheque? What for? She asked amazed.

'For the three divorces he didn't have,' Colleen laughed. Elaine was shocked when she saw the cheque.

'That's beyond belief,' she gasped. 'This just arrived for you, by the way.' She threw a pink envelope down on the desk.

Colleen picked it up slowly and opened it carefully.

'Dinner on Friday night,' she announced, happily.

'Oh my, girl, this is getting serious,' Elaine laughed.

'We will see Elaine.' Colleen picked up her coat and walked towards the door.

'Where are you going?'

'No idea, Elaine, I just have to walk.'

Richard and Ann were out walking with their children when one of the staff caught up with them.

'Excuse me, sir, this telegram was just delivered to the house for you,' he said, out of breath.

'Thank you Eric. There will be no reply just now.'

Richard opened it quickly and read it aloud to Ann. 'Sell the estate Richard, and come and live in Ireland. Signed: Thomas.'

Ann looked at Richard with a slight smile. 'What do you think of that?'

'I thought it was coming, my love. I just thought it would take him more time to make up his mind.'

'Are you happy about it?' she enquired.

'I think I am, Ann,' Richard sighed. 'This has been my home for a long time now but I actually felt more at home in Ireland.'

'So did I. Mary and I had become good friends and I was sad when we had to come back here.'

Richard picked up one of the girls. 'I think it's time for us to go back for tea.'

Ann took the hand of her other girl and they started walking back towards the house.

'One slight problem. I mentioned it to Simone last week that we might move back to Ireland, and she asked if she could come with us.'

'Oh that would be excellent, Richard. We have become very close friends. We have six bedrooms and she could come and live with us.'

'That's excellent for you, but there's just one problem.' Richard paused and looked serious. She would be a constant reminder of his ex-wife, because of the close resemblance. Do you think that that would cause a problem?

'Not at all, Richard. It was just the shock of meeting up for the first time, and I'm sure Thomas would be able to cope perfectly well.'

'I shall have to tell him, then.'

'I wouldn't Richard. Let's see how it all works out as the estate might not even sell.'

Thomas and Mary were having scones and coffee when Michael came downstairs. He said nothing as he pulled out the chair with his one good arm and picked out a scone. He tried to cut it with one hand but couldn't manage it. Mary came behind him and cut it for him then buttered it. 'Tea or coffee son?' she asked kindly.

'I'll try some of your American coffee, Ma, please, plenty of sugar.'

'Is you arm still sore, Michael?' Thomas asked, putting down his paper.

'It is, Da. It's very sore when I try and move it.' Michael replied, sheepishly.

'We thank God every day, Son; for looking after you. We could have been going to your funeral.'

'I wish I had been here for Dermot's funeral, Da. He didn't deserve to do die, you know?'

'None of us deserve anything in life, Michael. You've heard me say many times that we each have only a short time on this earth. None of us know when that time will end. That's why we must live each day like we only have one left. Only God knows why some of us live a short time and some a long time. It's a mystery that one day we will find out but for now we have to make each day count.'

'I've been given a second chance, Da, and I want to make the most of it.' Michael said, finishing his scone. 'I need to find something useful to do when my arm gets better.'

'You will, lad. Fist though, you must get better, and that starts by showing me this incredible boat you have built.'

They walked down to the pier to where the two boats were moored. 'The new one makes my boat look so old,' Thomas said, as he helped Michael climb in.

'Someone in Greencastle might buy it, Da.'

'I doubt it, Son. I think it's seen the end of its days. I installed the steam engine into it but it doesn't work very well.'

'Ours is great, Da, as John got an engineer in Derry at the boatyard to install it and show us how to work it.' Michael sounded happy for the first time since the shooting. 'You forgot to put an iron sheet under yours, Da, and if the hot coals had dropped out it might have set fire to the boat.'

Thomas reached over and looked into his old boat. 'Well, stone the crows, Son, you are quite right! I think we should take it out to sea and sink it.'

Just then they saw John arriving on his horse. 'Are you going to try it out?' he shouted to them as he tied the horse by the front door.

'We'll have to wait till the sailor's arm is better. We're just looking at this magnificent boat you both built me.'

'Well, it was my design and materials but it was Michael who did all the work,' he replied, as he walked towards them.

Thomas turned to Michael and gave him a big hug. 'Very proud of you, Son. Thank you so much.'

'The steam engine will take a bit of practice, but should take you in and out of The Foyle. It won't be strong enough at sea so you'll have to be sure to revert to sail.' John climbed into the boat.

'It uses a new type of fuel; a type of coal, but easier to store in this small cabinet', He opened a small wooden door and it was full of what looked like black stones. It'll give you enough steam for about four hours' sailing.'

'When Michael's arm is better, why don't we three take it for its maiden sail, then,' Thomas suggested eagerly.

'How are you Michael, anyway?' John asked, putting his hand on Michael's good shoulder.

'Just as well you didn't do that on my left shoulder, John,' Michael laughed.

It was getting dark by the time Colleen arrived, and John was just leaving. 'How's the one armed bandit?' she joked. Michael didn't reply, but gave her a slight smile.

'You're late again, Colleen,' Thomas scolded.

'Yes, Da. I had to go shopping for a new dress after work as I've been invited out for dinner tomorrow night.'

'Let me guess who invited you out then. Wouldn't be anyone by the name of David, by any chance?'

'Maybe,' smiled Colleen, as she walked in the front door.

'Hello, Ma. Would you have kept me a bowl of stew?'

'Good evening, Colleen, nice of you to come home. There might be a bit left over on the stove.' Mary watched her for a moment. 'You've a light step on ye tonight. It's as if something good had just happened,' she probed.

'No. Not much, Ma. We were handed a huge cheque today by one of my clients, and then I was invited out to dinner by the most handsome man in Derry. That's all,' she grinned.

'My advice, Daughter. Don't go too fast with that David. He seems a very nice young man, but I would be cautious of men with wealth.'

'The stew's really nice tonight, Ma,' Colleen answered, avoiding the comment.

Thomas and Michael came in just then and the conversation changed. Thomas looked at Colleen. 'Did you hear I have decided to sell my estate in England?'

'No, Da, I didn't. But that's a very big decision!'

'I think it's for the best right now and it'll pay for my next venture in Derry.'

'Will ye need a lawyer, Da?' Colleen laughed, as she put her empty stew plate in the sink.

'Can't think of one right now, girl,' Thomas smiled.

'Seriously though, Da, If you're thinking of starting another business in Derry, I would talk to David. He seems to be the person who can make anything happen in that city.'

'I'm going to bed,' Michael said, as he headed for the stairs.

'Will he be all right, Da?' Colleen asked, after Michael was out of hearing.

'He will, Colleen. It will take a while, but he'll come round.'

'Well if he needs any help I'll be here for him. Anyway, I'm off to bed.'

Chapter 14

William McFarland walked into his office, looking flustered. 'Where's Colleen?' he growled, as he made his way past Elaine.

'In her office, sir,' Elaine answered, timidly.

He pushed open Colleen's door. 'I've just met Andrew Watters in the town,' he started, as he slammed his briefcase down on the table. Colleen looked scared and sat back on her chair. 'He said you talked him out of his divorce.'

Colleen didn't know what to say. She thought she was about to be sacked.

'Why did you do that?' William barked.

'Because it was better for him, sir. He would have lost too much - in every way.'

'It was your job to keep him from losing too much, Miss Sweeney, and now we have probably lost him as our client.'

'How long did you talk to him for, sir?' Colleen asked quietly.

'We just passed in the street. He was in a hurry.'

'Did you ask him if he was pleased?'

'No, but he did mention that you were a brilliant lawyer,' he admitted.

Colleen reached into her desk drawer and brought out the cheque, handing it to William, who was now calming down. He looked at it for a few seconds. 'What's this?'

'That's Mr. Watters cheque. He was so pleased with my advice.'

'But this is for six hundred pounds!' he gasped.

'Yes. You told me to tell him it would cost two hundred pounds for his divorce. I told him that he still owed us for the last two attempts, so I presumed they would cost two hundred each as well.'

William sat speechless for a minute. 'Well, I must say then, Miss Sweeney, that this is some achievement! I must apologise. Forgive me for not checking the facts first. I don't know what to say.'

'You could let me finish early today as I have a dinner date with David Burns,' she smiled.

William lifted his briefcase from the desk and stood up. 'I'll do more than that, Colleen. On Monday I shall give you a pay rise and then start the process to get you trained properly.' He started to walk into his office but turned, 'I was going to try and get three hundred pounds out of the old gent, but you got six hundred! How on earth did you do that?'

Colleen just shrugged her shoulders and smiled.

'Six hundred pounds!' he muttered, walking away.'

Elaine came sneaking in the door when she heard the quiet, 'Are you all right, Colleen?'

'I'm fine, Elaine, thank you, but now I must get changed into my new dress.'

An hour later she walked out the front door of the office in her new formal dress. Everyone, without exception, stopped in the street to look at her. She enjoyed the attention as she waited for David's coach to collect her.

The coach arrived and she was about to open the coach door when David hopped out, opening it for her. Colleen's breath was taken away when she saw him. He was dressed in a full dinner suit and he looked so handsome that her heart missed a beat every time he looked at her with those dark eyes. David gave her a kiss on the cheek before helping her into the coach.

'I have never been across the river before, David. It's very pretty,' she said, gazing out the window.

'If you turn right at the end of the bridge you could see where we live. It's not far along that road. I'll take you there some day.'

She stared at all the shops as the coach went back along The Strand Road and was surprised when they went over the bridge which connected the city to The Waterside. She had never been across the bridge and began to get a bit nervous. Then they turned left at the end of the bridge and started going uphill.

Twenty minutes later, the coach arrived at a driveway with tall trees on each side, and eventually stopped at a magnificent house that looked like it was newly built.

David assisted Colleen in descending from the coach and she took his arm as they walked into the hotel. The foyer was magnificent, with cut-glass chandeliers and a marble floor. Colleen was fascinated by the new type of wall lights as well as the original paintings on the wall.

'I thought we would come here early, Colleen, as I'd like to drive you home before dark. I didn't think you'd feel comfortable taking the public coach home in an evening dress.'

'Very thoughtful of you, David, but we'll have plenty of time, as it doesn't get dark till about nine thirty.'

The meal was something that Colleen had only ever dreamed about. There were so many courses that she lost count of them. She had to ask David quietly what the knives and forks were for.

Dessert was finished, and the butler was pouring their coffee when David started very slowly.

'The reason I wanted to come early, Colleen, was, as I said, I'd love to drive you home. There's another motive behind my plan.' He smiled, leaning across the table and taking her hand. 'I'd like to speak with your father.'

'Really?' Colleen asked, 'For any particular reason?'

David just laughed, standing up and leading her out to the coach.

John was in the kitchen talking to Thomas. 'I've done more research for you, Thomas, and believe the idea of a button factory would be wonderful. If you give the go ahead I know of several buildings that would be perfect. You could have them up and running before the autumn and just in time for Richard to take over the running of it when he sells your estate.'

'Yes, provided it sells, John. It's now five and a half thousand acres of the best land in the county, but there are very few people in England who could afford such a large property.'

'Well, knowing Richard, he'll have no bother selling it.'

'I don't need a new business, John. I have so much money I don't even know how to spend it.'

'I know, Thomas, but your son needs it. His arm will be better soon and I worry about what he'll do then. He only got involved with that group because he needed something to do with a purpose. He's like his da. He can never sit at peace,' he smiled.

Thomas looked at John, grinning. 'Richard could give him a manager's job of some kind so that he feels he has achieved something.'

Thomas thought for a few minutes. 'Right, John. Off you go and find the right place.'

John got up from the table and was about to grab his coat when they heard a carriage stop at the front door. 'Who would that be at this time of the night?'

He opened the door to peer out and was surprised to see Colleen and David step out of the coach.

'It's your girl, Thomas. I'm away home now before Martha comes looking for me,' he laughed.

David and Mary acknowledged John and proceeded to walk straight on into the kitchen.

Thomas greeted them both and then beckoned to David to follow him into the living room.

'Where have you been?' he asked, sitting opposite him.

'We went for a meal in the city, and we came straight here afterwards.'

Then David decided to take advantage of this opportunity, and started. 'Mr. Sweeney. I love your daughter very much. She's the most wonderful, fun person I've ever met. We have so much in common. We both share the same interests. I just want to spend the rest of my life with her,' he said nervously. 'Mr. Sweeney, I would like to ask you if you would please grant me your permission to marry Colleen.'

Thomas went very quiet and looked closely at David for what, to him, seemed a lifetime. Suddenly a memory flashed across his mind. He remembered, in the same way, asking Lord Shrewsbury if he could marry his daughter. He had felt so incredibly nervous, but then, suddenly, the lord jumped up and exclaimed, 'Of course you can, Thomas!' He recalled the relief he'd felt at that moment.

'Of course you can, David!' he said, warmly, and reached for his hand.

David was surprised as he wasn't really expecting that reaction. He breathed a deep sigh of relief.

'I think we need a cup of tea, David.' Thomas said, calling Mary in.

'Thank you for the offer of tea, Mr. Sweeney, but I think I should go and ask Colleen if she might accept,' David said, as he moved to the kitchen door.

Colleen was chatting to her ma when David came in and took her by the hand. 'Colleen, would you like to go and watch the sunset, before I go?'

'Of course,' she smiled, happily.

While the sun was setting behind the house the moon had already appeared and was reflected on the still water.

'What were you talking to my da about? ' She asked, inquisitively.

Without answering he reached into his pocket and brought out a ring box. Getting down on one knee, he opened the box and showed her the ring. 'Colleen Sweeney. My one wish is to spend the rest of my life with you. You are the only person in this world for me. Will you marry me?' She smiled. 'Yes, David, I will.'

David stood up and slowly placed the ring on her finger. Then they kissed.

They stood for a long time watching the sea, their arms wrapped around each other.

'Shall we go and tell Ma now?' Colleen whispered, as the air was turning cold.

When they got back to the house Mary and Thomas were sitting side by side on the sofa. They looked like they were expecting them and, as they glanced at Mary's finger, they saw the sparkling ring.

'Congratulations, to you both!' Thomas laughed, jumping up to hug them both. Mary shook hands with David and then hugged her daughter, smiling broadly.

All four of them spent an hour chatting together about the future and wedding plans till Thomas said it was time for bed.

He turned to David 'You can't be driving your carriage home in the dark. Mary will show you to the guest room. I'll look after your horses.'

Colleen and Mary ran up the stairs with excitement to check the guest room while David turned to 'Thomas. Mr. Sweeney, I would also like to say that I believe I may be able to help you with your new business that you plan to start. I have a lot of properties and can pull a lot of strings in Derry so now that we are about to become related I would glad to help, sir.'

'Thank you, David. I'll certainly keep that in mind.' Thomas said, gratefully.

Chapter 15

The next morning was a Saturday and Mary made sure everyone was up for breakfast. The chatter amongst them all was about when a wedding might take place and where. They all agreed September would be a good month as Richard and Ann might have arrived by then.

'I would like the reception to be in the grandest hotel in Ireland,' David announced, finishing his eggs and toast. 'There's a new hotel called The Northern Counties in Portrush. It's supposed to be grander than any hotel in London or Paris, and by September the new railway line will be open.' Everyone nodded in agreement. 'I'll pay for everyone to stay there for the weekend. I'd be great to have all our families together.'

'Oh, no need for that, David,' Thomas said, smiling. 'I think we can afford to pay for our daughter's wedding.'

Colleen was about to respond when there was a knock on the door.

'Strange,' Mary said, going to open the door 'I didn't hear any horse or carriage.'

She opened the door and Sergeant O'Hare stood there, looking out towards the sea.

'Nice to see you again,' Mary said.

'Good morning folks. Nice to see a family all together eating breakfast. Brings me back to happier days when I was a wee boy.'

'Did you have a big family, Sergeant?' Mary asked, pouring him a cup of tea.

'Four brothers and five sisters.'

'Goodness, Alfred! Are they all still alive?'

'I lost a brother and a sister during the famine as they had moved away from Cork and ended up in a part of Galway that was badly affected. The others all left for distant shores. Some I hear from; some I don't.'

'Ireland was not a happy place during that time.' Thomas offered him a seat.

'No, it certainly was not. However, today I bring you some good news,' he said, helping himself to a scone.

'We have now officially decided that Michael will face no charges. The others will be up in court in Derry next month and I hope they go away for a long time.'

Michael looked down at the table and shifted nervously in his chair. 'The other news is that Dermot's family would like to meet you, Michael.'

Michael said nothing but looked nervous. 'Michael will call with them Alfred.' Thomas announced, decidedly.

The sergeant drank some tea and chatted with the family before getting up to go.

'I think it's time for me to get on the road as well,' David said. 'Thank you Mr. and Mrs. Sweeney for your kind hospitality. I'm certain we'll meet again soon.'

'I put your horses in the stables last night, David. I'll help you get them,' Thomas said, following him to the back door.

'I'm so glad to hear you're not going to be charged' Colleen said to Michael as she helped clear the breakfast dishes. Michael didn't reply but slowly got up from his seat and walked to the front door. He never looked back, closing the door gently behind him.

'He'll be all right, Colleen. Give him time to get over it all,' Mary said, quietly.'

'Do you believe that David is the right person, Colleen?' Mary asked, out of the blue.

'I believe so, Ma. He's a man of faith and principle; as well as being good fun and kind.'

'If you weren't in love, could you just be good friends?'

Colleen went quiet and thought for a minute. 'Yes, we're also good friends, Ma. We have a lot in common.'

'Then I believe you may have found the right one'

Just then the post-cart came to the front door and a man jumped out.

'I have a telegram for Mr. Sweeney, Ma'am,' he said, coming to the door. 'Will there be a reply?'

Mary took the envelope and opened it, glancing down. 'No that is fine, Seamus. Thanks very much.'

Colleen strained over her shoulder to try and read it.

'Have reached my home in Africa safely. Not many of my relations still alive. Thank you for your kindness. Charity.'

'Goodness! I'm not sure if I should tell Michael that this came. He has enough on his mind right now.'

2 months later

Richard and Ann's coach came to a stop at their front door. Simone and the children came out to meet them.

'Welcome home, sir,' Simone said, as the girls ran to their parents. 'I hope you had a good trip.'

'Not sure I'm very fond of London - or any city, for that matter, Simone. I think we made some progress though.' Richard hugged the children and walked up the steps.

'It would seem that there's some interest in the estate but it wasn't what was expected,' Richard laughed.

'Go on, tell her Richard,' Ann said, as she played with the children on the steps.

'Very well. We have had a small number of potential offers, but what came as a shock is an offer from Queen Victoria to buy the estate for the crown!'

'What? Are you serious?' Simone gasped. 'How on earth did she hear of the sale?.'

'I suppose she reads The Times newspaper too,' Richard smiled. 'The only problem is the offer is below our asking price.'

'It'll be difficult to sell such a large property, as many estate holders are finding it hard to keep such large houses and land, Ann joined in.

'Yes, but very few are as profitable as ours. We have a permanent electric generating station and a local water supply attached to it.' Richard sighed.

'I hope you don't mind, but I asked our chef to prepare dinner for you as I didn't know if you would have eaten,' Simone said.

'Well done, Simone. We're starving. Between trains and coaches it's a long journey from London.'

'Any word from Thomas?' Ann asked, as she handed the children to the nanny.

'Well, a very fancy looking envelope came yesterday by post. I put it on the mantelpiece in the living room.'

'Let's go and see then,' Richard said, walking towards the door.

'Goodness, that is a surprise!' he said, as he opened the gold coloured envelope. 'Thomas's daughter's getting married and we've all been invited on 22nd September to stay in The Northern Counties Hotel in a place called Portrush - wherever that is.'

'If we have sold this place by then, Richard, that would be about the time we would be arriving in Ireland anyway,' Ann said. 'I love weddings!' she said, happily.

Simone was standing looking very sad and turned her back to look out the window. Ann noticed and went over behind her. 'That includes you too, Simone.'

'I can't go to a wedding that I haven't been invited to, Anne,' she said, despondently.

'Now listen, Simone. Richard and I have talked at length and we have decided to ask you if you would like to come and live with us in Ireland. We have a huge house with eight bedrooms and we only need four. We would like you to be part of our family - only until you meet a fine Irish gentleman who takes you away to live in his castle, of course,' she laughed.

'I cant believe you would do that for me! You've only known me for six months and I haven't been able to offer you anything at all.'

'Oh you bring a lot more than you know, Simone. You have become a great friend in this lonely estate, and my girls adore you.'

They gave each other a hug. Then Simone thought, 'What about Thomas? I'm sure he wouldn't want me living next door to him and his wife. My being so like his former wife might stir too many memories.'

'It'll take him a little time, but I'm certain he'll get used to it. You are not Christina, you are Caroline - or Simone - and I'm sure you and Mary will get on just fine. One thing, though. We're not going to mention it to him. It will be a surprise,' Ann laughed, and went to the drinks cabinet.

Thomas was filling up the boat with coal for the engine when Michael appeared out of the front door. 'Ready for our maiden voyage, my son?' he shouted.

Michael walked over and looked down at the boat. 'What's the weather like today, Da?'

'It's grand, Son. There's a slight breeze, which we need for sailing, and, as far as I can see down the lough, the sea is calm. We'll only be going a short distance out anyway as I want to try the engine out.'

'Is John not coming with us? We promised him we'd take him on our first trip.'

'He's very busy right now organising a team for harvesting so we'll take him again some time.'

'Tell me when to let go the ropes, Da.'

'A few minutes, till we get plenty of steam going. We want to have plenty in case the wind's in the wrong direction.'

It took Thomas ten minutes to get the boiler red hot and then the steam valve started whistling.

'Right, son. Cast off and jump in,' he called.

Thirty minutes later they were well clear of the mouth of The Foyle and the sea was calm, with only a slight swell coming in from the North Atlantic.

'Right, Son. Let's try out the sails,' Thomas shouted to Michael, who was standing at the bow of the boat.

'Have you sailed before, Da?' Michael asked anxiously.

No, but it seems easy enough. We just hoist the main sail first then this smaller one at the back.

I followed the instructions my friend gave me and it's very simple to hoist the sails up and down.'

Michael stood beside Thomas and showed him what to do. 'If you pull this rope the sail goes up. You then tie it round the brass pin. To take it down you just release the rope and the sail will fall down again. Same with the back one.'

'Good. Leave them up and see what happens,' Thomas said, grabbing the tiller.

'You have to be careful with the back sail, Da, as it swings with the direction of the wind and could knock you into the sea if you aren't watching.'

'We'll only go a short distance as I want to be close to the shore in case of any problems.'

Within a few minutes the wind coming from the land filled the sails and the boat started to speed up. They were both sitting at the back while Thomas was having fun turning the boat from left to right with the tiller. The small waves were starting to break on the bow of the boat and the two of them sat contentedly looking out to sea.

'This is the life, Michael,' Thomas said. 'Blue skies, calm sea and wonderful sea air.' Michael moved to the bow again to look over at the boat cutting through the sea.

Thomas left the tiller for a second while he closed the drought on the engine fire door. As he stood up suddenly the wind caught the back sail and swung in across the boat. The beam hit Thomas on the head and he fell to the deck.

Michael sat for a few minutes enjoying the spray starting to come over the bow, but when he looked back he was horrified to see his da was not at the helm.

'Da,' he screamed, 'Where are you? He ran to the back of the boat and found his father lying flat on his face on the deck.

Thomas shook him. 'Da! Wake up! Wake up! Are you all right?'

There was no response. Michael shook him harder and began to cry, 'Da, please, wake up! Wake up!'

Michael turned his da's head round and could see blood coming from a gash. 'Oh no,' he prayed, crying so hard he could hardly see. He suddenly realised that the boat was still heading out to sea. 'How do I turn this thing?' he said to himself, in a panic. 'I have to get home urgently!'

He ran to the small sail and untied the rope so that it fell down. Pushing the beam out of the way, he grabbed the tiller. He pushed it hard to the left and was relieved when the boat started to turn.

It was a long slow turn, and now the wind was against the boat and it started to slow down. He realised that the wind would eventually stop him getting back up the river. Michael straightened the boat up and tied a piece of rope around the tiller to keep it straight. He then climbed over his father and pulled the main sail down. The only way to get home now was by using the engine, so he climbed to the back of the boat again. Looking at the firebox, he could see that the draught was closed, but he burnt his hand opening it as he didn't know about the metal rod for moving it. As soon as he opened the draught he could see the fire start to go red again. He pushed the drive leaver forward, but nothing happened. Michael remembered his da saying that the fire had to build up steam before it would drive the boat. All he could do was wait and pray. He looked out over the side of the boat to see if there were any other boats who might come to his rescue. Seeing that the fishing boats were all in the harbour, he went back to his da and looked helplessly at him as he lay there.

'God, please, let my da live,' he prayed, as he stroked his face.

Suddenly he heard the steam whistle sound, which meant there was enough steam for the engine so he tried the drive leaver again and this time the boat started to move forward slowly.

It was the longest hour in his life, but eventually he saw his own pier in the distance. He put the last shovel of coal in the boiler, hoping desperately that it was enough to cover the last half mile. Michael looked at his da, still lying still. His stomach was sick, and he wondered how he was going to tell everyone that his da was dead. He could hardly see ahead with the tears blinding him. He put more coal in the boiler and was surprised at how fast the boat was now moving. He kept looking over at his da hoping he would wake up, when suddenly he thought he saw him move. Jumping down from the tiller, he knelt beside him. Just then, Thomas slowly opened his eyes.

'Da,' Michael shouted, as he tried to hold his head up.

'Where am I?' Thomas mumbled, groaning.

'You're on the boat, Da, and you got hit on the head by the moving mast. I thought you were dead.'

'Not yet, Son, but my head is very sore.' He tried to sit up but fell back down again.

'I thought we were gone. I didn't know how to get the boat back home.' Michael was crying again.

'Careful, Michael! You're heading for the rocks!' Thomas managed, groggily.

Michael jumped back to the tiller and swung the boat back on course for their pier. As the boat approached their house. Michael started shouting for help. No one came at first but as they came within fifty yards of the pier he saw John running from the house.

John grabbed the rope that Michael threw to him while shouting,

'What happened?' Then he saw Thomas lying in the boat and quickly jumped in. He helped Thomas stand up.

'I don't think I'm cut out to be a sailor, John,' Thomas said, weakly. 'That stupid mast nearly killed me.'

'The beam swung round with the wind and nearly knocked my da into the sea,' Michael said.

'Oh my goodness, Thomas! How many lives have you got?'

John helped them both out of the boat, before Mary came running to them.

'Michael saved us both, John. He got the boat turned and managed to get the sails down before bringing us safely home with the engine. He's my hero,' he said proudly.

Mary arrived and helped John take Thomas back to the house. 'We'll need to get a doctor to check his head, Mary,' John said, 'That's a nasty gash.'

'What were you doing here anyway, John?' asked Thomas, curiously.

'I don't know, Thomas. I was at home when I got this sudden urge that I should come and visit you. I just left it a bit late as I could have come on your boat trip'.

Thomas looked at him and smiled.

Chapter 16

Richard was pacing up and down the great hall at the front of the house. Everything that he could think of was ready, and the staff were well prepared. Ann appeared from the kitchen. 'Do you think she'll like parsnip soup and roast beef?' she enquired, as she took Richard's arm.

Richard was almost too nervous to answer. 'We should never had agreed to feed her. What an upheaval - and what a cheek! Imagine sending some her own chefs to cook in our house! I find that very insulting.'

'Never worry, Richard. I hear the queen does that wherever she travels. It's probably a tradition from the past when they used to try and poison the kings and queens of England.'

'I hope no local people know that Queen Victoria is coming here today. It would destroy our reputation.'

'What are you talking about, Richard? What reputation?'

'Our reputation of not being snobs in our big house; something which I've tried very hard to work on for the past 20 years.

Ann looked out the window. 'Oh my goodness! There's a carriage now. Oh my! It looks like about six carriages! Perhaps she's planning to stay! Richard ran to the door but then stopped. 'Andrew!' he called, in a panic. 'The queen is here!'

The carriages drew up at the front door, with the second one stopping at the bottom of the steps.

A butler opened the door and the queen stepped down from the coach. The butler bowed. Other people in fine clothes then appeared behind her.

Andrew approached the queen, bowing. 'Your Majesty. Welcome to Shrewsbury Hall.'

The queen waited till her own groom was beside her. 'Thank you. I shall take a quick look at the gardens first before we go in as the weather is so pleasant'

Richard rushed down the steps when he saw she wasn't coming straight in, and went to join her. 'Your Majesty. I am Richard Smith. May I welcome you to my home,' he stuttered, nervously.

The queen said nothing, but continued towards the fountains and gardens. She was dressed in a long black dress, and Thomas was taken by how small she was. 'The fountains were designed by the late Lady Christina Shrewsbury, Your Majesty.'

'When did your wife die?' Richard noticed a tone of disinterest.

'She was not my wife, Ma'am. The wife of the owner, Thomas Sweeney.

'Why is the owner not here to show me his estate?' She asked, looking annoyed.

'He's in Ireland on business, Your Majesty, and he asked me to show you around.'

'Hmph.' She turned and walked back to the house. ' I would like to view your dining room now, if you do not mind.'

Richard and the entourage followed behind as the queen walked back to the steps where Ann was waiting to greet her.

'Welcome to our home, Your Majesty,' Ann said, bowing.

'You are not in Ireland with your husband, then?' She murmured, as she brushed past her.

Ann didn't even have time to reply but joined Richard in following her into the dining room.

The queen looked round at the Shrewsbury family paintings before sighing. 'I knew Lord Shrewsbury. In fact, we were related. He was a wonderful character. I was in this house a long time ago.' She walked over to the window over-looking the garden and stood staring out for about a minute before turning towards the door. 'That's fine. I shall take it,' she announced, decisively.' My people will be in touch shortly to sort everything out.' She then moved towards the front door before Richard stammered apologetically. 'I'm sorry, Your Majesty ... but ... aren't you staying for lunch?'

'No thank you', she stated crisply. 'I merely came to view the property.'

They all followed her down the steps and the valet helped her into the coach. Within a minute the entire entourage was gone and Richard and Ann just stood and stared as if they had just been part of some strange theatre production.

'I'm so glad I'm moving to Ireland, Ann,' Richard said, as he shook his head. 'I've never met a more pompous person in my life.'

'Well she is The Queen of England, Richard. She's expected to be a little bit pompous, is she not?'

'Manners,' Richard said, as he turned back to the house. 'A little bit of manners never hurt anyone - whether they're queen or not. Anyway, I'm going to invite the staff to eat the lunch that she left. They can have a real feast to themselves,' he said, happily, rubbing his hands.

'Good. Well, you'd better let Thomas know straight away that the house is sold.'

Colleen came home after work to find her da lying on the sofa with his head bandaged and looking sorry for himself.

'What happened, Da?' she cried, as she ran to his side.

'Awe not much, really. Just got a wee bang on the head when our boating trip went wrong.'

'I thought you didn't like boats...but, what happened?'

Thomas related the story to Colleen while Mary fetched her dinner from the oven.

'I forgot to tell you, Thomas, with all the excitement…two telegrams came for you while you were out at sea.' Mary sounded flustered.

Thomas frowned as Mary handed the envelopes for him to open.

'Richard has just sold my estate to Queen Victoria, and he's arriving here next month!' he announced excitedly.

'Is that a joke?' Colleen asked, as she started eating her dinner.

'Apparently not. He got my asking price. What that means, is that none of us will need to work for a very long time.'

'There will be a huge tax bill on that, Da,' Colleen piped up.

'I know, and I also have to pay Simone a large amount as well.'

'Why do you have to do that? Why give your money to a stranger?'

'Because she's the real daughter of Lord Shrewsbury and Christina's twin sister.'

'Who is the other telegram from?' Mary asked.

'A wee surprise, my love. Trust me. I can't say at present. All will be revealed in good time.' Thomas said mysteriously, as he crumpled the telegram and threw it in the open fire.

'David asked could he come and see you on Saturday, Da. He has some interesting options for your business but said he would need a few hours to talk to you.'

'Saturday's fine, Colleen, as long as my head's working by then,' he laughed.

Mary went out the back door. Thomas called Colleen over beside him to tell her about the telegram and they talked quietly for a few minutes before Mary came back. She seemed pleased with what Thomas told her, but added quietly. 'I'll need to ask David on Saturday. I'm sure he'll be fine with your plan.'

Michael arrived in Moville on his favourite horse, the big black hunter. He turned right and rode for a mile out the Carndonagh Road before he came to a lane on his right, with a steep climb up towards an old farmhouse.

As he dismounted at the front door he felt sick with nerves. A man dressed in working clothes and a flat cap came to the door. Michael reckoned he was around fifty, but looked much older as he was stooped over and had a very weather-beaten face.

'Pardon me, sir. Is this Gallagher's?' he asked quietly

'It is, indeed. I'm Sean Gallagher ... and I presume you must be Michael Sweeney. Come on in.'

He led him into the front room which was a combined kitchen and living room. His wife appeared from a small room at the back. 'This is Michael, Breege. Our Dermot's friend.'

They all sat down at the kitchen table while Breege made tea.

Michael looked down at the table. He didn't know where to start.

'Thank you for coming. Dermot talked very fondly of you.'

'I don't know how to say sorry,' Michael said quietly, his head still bowed. 'I should have persuaded him to run away.'

'It would have made no difference, Son. Those evil men had it all planned that if anyone was to be caught it would be you two. They were cowards.'

'He was such a good lad. You should be very proud of your son,' Michael said sadly.

'We heard from the police their side of the story and was wondering if yours was any different,'

Sean asked, as Breege poured the tea.

'We came out the door thinking we just had to drop the guns in a cart at the end of the path. I was carrying three rifles and Dermot could only manage two. They were very heavy and he dropped his at the door. He had just picked them up again and was trying to hold them on his shoulder when the shooting started. He never had a chance.'

'I wish I could do something to make it up to you,' he said, sadly.

'It was very brave of you to come,' Sean said, 'and it means a lot to us right now. Thank you, Son. We miss Dermot so much. Did he ever tell you that when he was younger he always said that he'd like to join the police one day? We just can't believe the way things turned out.'

Michael was very upset and stood up to leave. He headed for the door with tears in his eyes.

All the way back to Moville he couldn't stop thinking about Dermot. He was surprised at his parents telling him about him wanting to join the police. He couldn't get it out of his head. Why hadn't Dermot ever told him this? He tried to imagine Dermot in a police uniform - and even himself as well, standing beside him.

Michael had made up his mind. He turned left to go up the main street to the police station, but just then all the past events came flooding back to him and he nearly ran back down the path. Nevertheless, he continued. He stopped at the front door before pushing it open and, upon entering, he cautiously approached the policeman was standing behind a counter. 'Can I help you?' he asked.

'I would like to speak to Sergeant O'Hare, please,' Michael said softly.

The police man disappeared out a door behind the counter and then returned with the Sergeant.

'Hello Michael,' he started. 'How's your arm?'

'Fine thank you, sir.' Michael moved nervously.

Alfred came around the counter and took Michael gently by the arm to some seats by the window.

'This must be very hard for you, son, coming in here,' he said very gently.

Michael just nodded.

'It will take a long time to get over something like that, Michael, so don't try and rush things.'

'I have been thinking, Sergeant, maybe in the future I might join up.'

'That's a big decision, Michael. It's not something I would rush into, considering past events.'

'I understand,' Michael said, standing up. 'It's something I had thought about for a while.'

'If you decide, Michael, then I would need to convince my superiors. Good luck for now, Son.'

Michael turned and walked back to his horse.

Colleen was standing at the entrance to their driveway waiting for David's coach to appear. She was getting excited as it was only a month till her wedding. They had difficulty trying to work our which church they would get married in. They decided that it would be easier for everyone if they got married in a small church in Portrush so everyone could walk to the hotel. David had long discussions with his father, but in the end he was just glad to see his thirty year old son finding the right person. David and Colleen had agreed to the secret that Thomas had mentioned. The coach arrived on time and stopped beside her.

'Excuse me, miss,' David started, in a mock posh accent. 'Can you tell me the way to the Sweeney castle. I hear there's a banquet on today.'

'Just give me a lift, cheeky, and we might find you a piece of scone bread,' Colleen laughed, as she climbed into the carriage.

They hugged and kissed all the way to the front door.

Thomas and John were standing talking looking at the pier when the coach pulled up.

'Good to see you, sir,' David said, jumping down. 'Tis a fine summer we are having.'

'Thank you for coming. David,' Thomas replied laughing, 'although I didn't need too much persuasion to come this way.' Colleen jumped down behind him.

'I think we could have our meeting outside today if that suits you.'

'Certainly. I love watching the sea.'

The four of them sat down by the wooden picnic table, when David said, 'I think Colleen should join us in our meeting, gentlemen, as we might need her legal advice,' he said, beckoning Colleen to join them. Thomas and John looked a bit surprised, but said nothing.

'Now, Mr. Sweeney,' David started, with a formal voice. 'I have discussed your plans with my father and we've come up with an idea that, I hope, might suit you.'

He opened a large sheet he had brought with him which showed plans of a building.

'My father has a number of large properties that could be made into a factory. When you mentioned that you thought you might have a staff of twenty five to fifty and that you needed access to plenty of fresh water, we narrowed it down to this one. It is on The Strand Road in Derry. It's outside the city walls, opposite the end of the docks. It would be handy for any materials that you might be shipping in, and it could also have a pipe going in and out of the river.' He paused and turned the plan over to reveal the location of the building. My father said that, because I'm marrying into your family, the building will be a gift.'

They all sat in silence, considering the enormity of this generous offer. Eventually, Thomas turned to John. 'What do you think John? You're the only one of us who has ever been in a button factory.'

'I think it is ideal, and, if I may say, a very generous offer by Mr. Burns. I would prefer to pay something for it, David, to keep things right.' Thomas looked up from the plans.

He turned to Colleen. 'And what does the lawyer think?'

'Well, I'm not sure,' Colleen replied, with a mischievous tone. ' I think a lawyer, at great expense, is required to check the contracts.'

They all laughed. 'Please thank your father for his generous offer, David, and once the wedding is over, we shall be glad to discuss this in more detail.' Thomas stood up.

Chapter 17

Richard, Ann, Simone and the girls stood in a line at the front of the dining room facing all their staff. Their baggage was already in the two carriages. Everyone was very sad and it wasn't going to be easy for Richard to announce his farewell to his staff. He cleared his throat and kept his handkerchief in his hand.

'Good morning, everyone. This is a very sad day for us. I want to thank each of you for your service to Thomas's family and my own for the last twenty years. We always considered each one of you more as family than employees. We have shared happy and sad times together. It's without question that it is you, folks, who have made this estate one of the best in England. Thomas has decided to sell the estate because he believes that it will become more difficult in years to come to keep a house of this size going. The house also holds too many memories for him to ever return here. As most of you know, we have sold the estate to The Crown. I have requested that all of you are kept in employment. However, not all of you may wish to work for The Royal Family as their way of working will be very different from ours. Our house manager, Andrew, has already told us he's going to retire, and I'm sure you will join with me in wishing him every happiness for his future.' He paused and, walking over to the table, he picked up a pile of envelopes. 'There's an envelope here for every member of staff, regardless of the position you hold. Thomas has put cash in each envelope for you in thanks for your service. I hope the money will help you start a new life should you chose to leave here. I have only one last thing to say and that is simply to say thank you to you all. You have all become my dearest friends.'

Richard moved to give out the envelopes and shake everyone's hand.

Andrew then stopped him and turned to face the staff. 'I think I have the right to speak for everyone, sir, when I say that we have been honoured to serve such a kind family. We never felt that we were servants and we must have been the most blessed staff in all of England. We will miss your family - and Thomas - immensely. We wish you all a very happy life in Ireland and hope that one day we will meet again.'

Richard wiped a tear from his eye as he turned to talk to the people standing around.

It took nearly half an hour to say goodbye, but eventually it was time to get into their luxurious carriage one last time. All the staff came out to wave them goodbye, and everyone was in tears as they set off down the driveway.

There wasn't much chat out of any of them during the long train journey to Liverpool. They arrived at the harbour for six pm. The girls were exited as they had never been on a train or ship before - thus lightening the atmosphere.

The ship sailed at eight, and they all stood on the rear deck to say goodbye to England. Richard and Ann held hands as Simone played with the girls. The sun was setting as the ship sailed out of the lough, and Richard and Ann decided they would go below decks to their cabin. Simone asked if she could stay on her own as she wanted to reflect on the life-changing events which had taken place since the time she knocked on the door of the grand house. She walked along the starboard deck to the front of the ship where the wind was gently blowing her hair. Taking deep breaths of the fresh salt air, she was unaware of a tall, handsome man who was doing the same thing behind her. He was dressed in a fashionable suit with an expensive long overcoat. His dark brown eyes were magnified by a neat trimmed moustache and he was gazing out to sea absent-mindedly when he suddenly turned his head and looked at Simone. She glanced shyly at him then turned away. As she looked back again, a strange feeling coming over her. She had never felt like this in her life before and felt scared because it was as if some unknown power was causing her to be drawn to this man. She got nervous and sighed as she didn't have the courage to speak to him and, as she went to walk away, the man spoke.

'Are you leaving home, too?' he asked in a soft Irish accent.

Stopping in her tracks, she turned towards him and spoke slowly. 'I don't really know where my home is, sir. I'm leaving England for a new life in Ireland.'

He said nothing and just stared at the beautiful woman standing before him. Simone glanced up at him and she felt her heart jump. The wind had blown her hair into her face so she brushed it away.

'That sounds like you've had some sadness in your life, Ma'am,' the man ventured.

'I've had a good life, with some sad times, just like anyone else. My new life is about to start now, so I'm hoping there will be good times ahead.'

'Oh, and how has that come about?' the man asked, moving closer towards her.

'I've found some wonderful new friends who helped me to find out who I really am. Now I'm going to live with them in Ireland,' Simone said, as she moved her hands nervously.

'That sounds very interesting. Do you know what part of Ireland you're going to live in?'

'I believe it is near a town called Moville in Donegal, wherever that is.'

The man smiled as he pulled a cigarette out of his inside pocket. 'Donegal is the most northerly part of Ireland. I live about twenty miles away from Moville in a village called Buncrana.'

'My! That's a real coincidence, sir!' Simone exclaimed. 'So we could end up being neighbours.'

'I choose my neighbours very carefully,' the man joked. 'May I ask the lady's name?'

'Simone. And you are...?'

'Patrick Gallagher at your service, Ma'am.' He took her hand and kissed it. 'Simone is a French name, is it not?'

'Yes. My mother was Renee, from Paris, who came to work in England before I was born,' she answered, as she turned and looked out to the sea again.

'I see you're shivering, Simone. Perhaps it's time to say goodbye to England and go inside.'

Simone turned back and smiled at Patrick and, a little too hastily, asked, 'Excuse me, but will we meet again, Patrick?' She immediately regretted being so forward.

'We might, Simone. You never know which way the wind blows.' He gave a warm smile.

Simone suddenly realised that she didn't even have an address to give him. 'I believe our house is in the grounds of a Mr. Thomas Sweeney. He's well known locally, so perhaps you might look us up one day,' she said with a burning feeling in her heart.

'I'll look forward to that, Simone,' Patrick answered, smiling as he took her hand. 'I hope you get some sleep tonight as this crossing can sometimes get a bit rough.' Patrick kissed her hand again and bid her goodnight.

Simone was so full of emotions she got lost trying to find her way to her cabin and had to ask several seamen on the way. She had never felt this way before. She had had two previous suitors but never knew what real love was. She had just felt used, in a way. This man was different. When their eyes met it was if he could see into her soul. She was glad to close her cabin door and just lay awake on her bed thinking of this charming Irish man who seemed so mysterious and yet so kind.

Chapter 18

Thomas and Mary spent all morning cleaning Richard and Ann's house to have it ready for them. Thomas lit all the fires, even though August was still warm. He had his gardener trim back the hedges and trees that had overgrown in the two years they had been in England. Thomas had made a wooden sea-saw for the girls. He was so pleased that his best friend was finally going to be living beside him.

'The girls must be coming five and four,' Mary said as she gathered up her bag of clothes.

'They're getting big, and take after their mother in looks and personality. I'm really looking forward to having them here - till we get some grandchildren of our own, that is' Thomas laughed.

'What time will they arrive?'

'I sent our coach to Derry to pick them up from the train, so they should be here in another hour.'

Just then John appeared on his horse. 'I thought I might find you here,' he said, dismounting. 'Martha's very anxious to know when Richard's coming. She's looking forward to having new friends for our children.'

'Yes. The quiet life I dreamt of is slowly disappearing - only this time without me going anywhere,' Thomas smiled.

'I sincerely hope you never leave these grounds again. I think we're all glad your adventures are over.'

'No they're certainly not over, John,' Thomas said laughing. 'Life is one big adventure.'

'David asked me to go and look at the building with him. I just wanted to check with you in case you would like to see it too.'

'I would wait a week and then take Richard with you as I don't intend to have anything to do with it. It'll be his project to keep him busy,' Thomas said, as he started walking back to his own house.

'Did Thomas get over the boat incident, Mary?' John asked, when Thomas was out of ear shot.

'I think it finished him with the sea, John. His heart was only in it to help Michael. I hope now that he'll find something to do. ' Mary answered. 'It could have easily been another tragedy.'

'Maybe you could ask Thomas some day if he would like me to sell the boats. It would be a shame to see them rot away at your pier.'

Thomas and Mary were surprised when the coach arrived early at their door. The two of them ran out the front door as Richard was helping Ann climb down from the coach. Next, the two girls appeared - followed by Simone. Thomas was so shocked he couldn't speak. Mary saw his face and tried to make light of the situation. Richard was clearly embarrassed. It was Ann who broke the awkward silence.

'This is our very good friend, Simone,' she announced, with a big smile.' She's going to live with us until she can find her own life and home in Donegal.'

Simone went forward and shook Mary's hand. 'I've heard a great deal about you, Simone,' Mary said, warmly. 'You're very welcome here, and I hope you will be very happy in Donegal.'

Thomas nodded his head politely.

'Everyone in for tea,' Mary shouted. They all went towards the front door.

Richard pulled Thomas aside. 'Sorry, Thomas. This was Ann's idea. I tried to discourage her, but hopefully she will find her own house as soon as possible. Maybe some distance away.'

'No. I'm fine. Really. I was just a bit shocked to see her here,' he said, as they walked in the door.

Michael was sitting on the edge of their pier looking at the boat that he had built. The sun was setting and the sea was as calm as glass. He was thinking about how lucky Colleen was to be getting married next month. He sighed, but as he gazed out over the water, he heard someone come up behind him. He didn't look around as he didn't want to spoil his quiet moment.

'What a beautiful evening,' a familiar voice said.'

Thomas looked around and gasped. 'Charity!'

She had tears in her eyes, but managed a gentle smile.

'What ...? How did you get here ... I mean ... when did you arrive?' Thomas spluttered.

'I've been staying with Richard and Ann for two days. I wanted to surprise you.'

'Why did you come back, Charity?' Michael asked, seriously. 'Were none of your family still alive?'

'I found a few uncle and aunts, but they weren't interested in me. I couldn't stop thinking about you and how wrong I was to leave you just before our wedding.' She wiped her tears away with her sleeve. 'Can you ever forgive me, Michael?'

Michael looked closely into her eyes. He didn't speak right away. Eventually, he took her hand in his. 'I will only forgive you, Charity,' he said, getting down on one knee, 'If you will marry me.'

Charity leant forward and hugged him 'Of course I will, and this time I won't run away, not now - and not ever,' she smiled, happily.

They hugged, cried and talked together till the sun set.

As the sun was going down, Thomas happened to be out walking and saw them sitting there. He came up behind them. 'Ah. I see you found him then,' he said, softly.

Michael turned to his da. 'You knew about this, Da?'

Charity answered before his da could reply. 'Your da paid for me to come back home, Michael'.

Michael went over and hugged his da tightly. 'Thank you so much, Da. You're the best ever'.

'I think we should go in now. It's getting a bit chilly,' Thomas said, putting his arm around them both. 'I have an idea.' He paused, before asking, 'Why don't we have a double wedding next month - provided David and Colleen would be happy with that arrangement - but keep it a surprise?'

Michael and Charity looked at each other and laughed, excitedly. 'That sounds like a great idea,' they both said together.

During the next three weeks, life was very busy at their house as they were making last minute plans for the wedding and helping Richard and Ann settle back into their home. Simone loved children. Now she had four to play with, as John and Martha came to their house nearly every day. David's father signed over a lot of his business to him, making him one of the wealthiest young men in the country.

Colleen was given two weeks off and spent most of it in Derry and she and David were busy buying things for their future house which they had just bought in a townland called Fahan.

Mary had to persuade Bridget and Rose to make the long train journey as they had never been out of Donegal in their lives. She also had to tactfully persuade them to buy a few new dresses to fit in with changing fashions.

In the meantime, Colleen was busy helping Charity pick a wedding dress from Austins Department store. They spent a lot of time together talking about the uprise that people would get on their wedding day.

Chapter 19

Simone decided one afternoon, while walking on the beach just past the house, that she would begin exploring the area. It was a typical September day; still mild, but with crisp fresh air blowing gently off the river. The sky was a deep blue, and she noticed quite a number of sailing boats going up and down the river. She was very content and happy to be starting a new life and, as she stopped to pick up a shell, she heard a voice from behind.

'Pretty here, isn't it?' Thomas said.

She turned, startled. 'Oh! Hello Thomas.'

'Were you dreaming?' he asked, as walked towards her.

'No. Not exactly. My dreaming days are over. I'm so contented being here in Donegal.'

Thomas smiled. 'Some day a very lucky man will find you as his wife, Simone. I hope he'll be someone who is very special, for that's what you deserve.'

'My sister was the luckiest woman in the world to have been married to you, Thomas. I wish I had been there to see how happy she must have been.' She sat down on a large rock.

'She was my life, Simone. She would have loved to have known she had a younger twin sister. The two of you could have had a great life together. It was so desperately sad that your mother was not well enough to keep you.' Thomas sat beside her on the rock.

'We might have fought over you,' Simone laughed. 'No, it was never meant to be, and I've had a good life.'

'Did you know that you had a brother as well?'

Simone turned to him, quickly. 'What? A brother? Oh my goodness!

Why didn't anyone tell me this before? Where is he now?'

'Edward died about five years ago, I'm afraid, after a very sad life. I'll tell you about it some day. This isn't the right time,' Thomas said, standing up.

Simone stood up and walked towards the water, clearly upset at this latest news. Thomas stood and watched her, feeling sad for her.

'You are a very kind and decent man Thomas. It's an honour to know your family, and I thank you for being so kind to me.'

'Your family meant so much to me, Simone, and I would have nothing in this life without them. That's why I must look after you now,' Thomas smiled, 'And, of course, you're now just like one of our family.'

'That makes me very happy, Thomas,' Simone said, 'I would also love to have a deeper faith, like you.'

'And so you shall, Simone. So you shall. Now let's go and get some tea.'

They walked slowly back to the house.

On the way back, Simone stopped suddenly and turned to Thomas, blushing slightly. 'I want to tell you something: I met a man whom I think I've fallen in love with.'

Thomas stopped and looked back at her. 'Really?' he said, surprised. 'Who is he?'

'I met him for twenty minutes on the Liverpool boat. Our hearts met as if we were the only two people in the world.'

Thomas shook his head. 'You must find him then. That is how your sister and I felt when we first met. Our hearts met in our eyes. It only happens once in a lifetime.'

'If it's meant to be, then we will find each other again,' she sighed.

'Simone.' He paused and looked closely at her. 'You will find him.'

They came to the end of the beach, and had just started to walk on the garden path when Simone froze. Walking up the driveway towards the house was the man she was talking about.

'Thomas! That's him!' She said, in shock, wiping the hair from her face.

'That's who?' Thomas frowned.

'The man I met on the ship!' Simone was breathing heavily.

Thomas reached down and squeezed her hand. 'Run, girl, run,' he laughed.

Simone walked fast until she was a few feet from the man. He stopped, transfixed, and then smiled. Simone walked towards him with a huge smile on her face. 'You came?' she said, softly.

The man shrugged his shoulders and smiled. 'I had to try and find you,' he replied, with a sparkle in his eye as he began walking towards her slowly until they were almost touching. 'I don't know who you, are but I would love to get to know you better.'

Simone moved close to him and looked up into his eyes. Thomas was standing watching and gave a quiet cough. They turned and laughed. 'Thomas, this is Patrick,' she said, as she led him by the hand towards the house.

'It is nice to meet you Patrick. I think we need that tea now, Simone.'

The day before the wedding everyone made the journey by train to Portrush. The summer weather had returned and it was warm and sunny. Everyone was greatly impressed at the grandeur of The Northern Counties Hotel. The reception area, with its cut-glass chandeliers, looked as grand as any palace in the country. Richard commented that it was even grander than his house back in England.

Thomas had invited many of the local people from Greencastle and Moville. He had questioned Patrick at length that night when they met and found out that he was a teacher at a prestigious school in London. His wife had died a year ago and Patrick had lost his desire to stay in a big city, longing instead to return to his home village of Buncrana. He told Thomas he thought he would never fall in love with another woman after being with the love of his life for twenty years. That was until he met Simone on the ship. He said he had fallen in love with her at first sight. Thomas explained that he had done the same when he first met her sister, Christina. He explained about Simone's past, which came as a shock to Patrick, but made him love her even more. Thomas invited him to the wedding and now they walked side by side down by the sea.

'Have you thought about your future. Patrick?' Thomas asked, as they watched the waves crashing on the strand.

'I would love to get a teaching post locally, but that might take time, as the country is still recovering from the famine.'

'I will be giving Simone an inheritance, but wanted to make sure she found someone who wouldn't take advantage of her.'

'I have my own wealth, sir, as I sold my house in London for a substantial profit but, to be honest, I'm not very materialistic. Money doesn't interest me much. My desire is to educate young Irish people so that they will never be forced to rely on the British government for their life again. It's time to create a nation of independent workers, as we have a large pool of talent here on our own soil just waiting to be discovered.'

Thomas turned and shook his hand, satisfied that Simone had found a good man.

They walked back to the hotel as Thomas wanted to talk to David. He found him talking to his relations in the lounge, where Thomas was introduced to his parents.

After dinner that evening Thomas took Mary by the arm and walked on the strand at the front of the hotel. 'It is hard to believe I will be losing my wee girl tomorrow,' Mary said sadly.

'Ah sure she is only on loan to David, till God takes her home.' Thomas replied, as he breathed in the evening fresh sea air. 'I'm so pleased for Michael too, though. It's hard losing them both on the one day.'

'All the guests are going to get some shock, Thomas. Do you not think we should have told them?'

The two couples are still keen on the idea of a double wedding, Mary, so let's not say anything.'

'I must go and see Colleen. This will be the last night she will be my little girl. Tomorrow she will belong to another person,' Mary said sadly. Thomas walked Mary back to the hotel.

Colleen was rushing around her room looking for a hair slide she had lost when Mary came in.

'Are you all right, sweetheart,' Mary said, picking up some of the clothes lying on the floor.

'Can't find the gold hair slide, Ma,' she shouted.

'Calm down, daughter. We'll find it. It's not like you to panic about anything.'

'I know. Ma, but this is the first time that I've got married!' Colleen said, flustered.

Mary came over and sat down behind her. She picked up the gold slide from the floor. 'Is this what you're looking for?'

Colleen sighed. 'Where would I be without my ma?' she said, giving her a hug and wiping a tear from her eye.

'Where I will always be, Colleen. Just like my ma was for me. Tomorrow you and David will be a married couple, but you always be my little Colleen - till the day I die.'

Colleen turned and hugged her again. 'Where would I be without the best parents in the world?'

'Are you sure David is the one for you, my love?'

Colleen went quiet and looked searchingly into her ma's eyes. 'I believe so, Ma - I know he is. We're such good friends and share so much in common - including our faith.'

Mary hugged her daughter again, with tears in her eyes.

The chapel on the main street was packed with three hundred guests. It was a long time since the town had had so many wealthy visitors, and many local people were standing out at the front door waiting for the bride. David, dressed in a very expensive suit, looked very handsome. Michael was standing at his right side feeling nervous. The congregation assumed that he and the man standing beside him were David's two best men, totally unaware that Michael was also about to become a bridegroom. The families all looked so happy and were all dressed in their splendour, sporting the very latest fashions from Austins Department Store.

Then the priest appeared from a door at the back and came and stood at the front.

'Ladies and gentlemen, I would like to give you all a very warm welcome to our wedding service this morning. I would especially like to welcome the many people have come from other faiths to join us today. Also the many people who have travelled a long distance to be here; especially one person - who has come from the other side of the world.' He paused to watch the people's reaction, but no one seemed to sense what he was about to say.

'Ladies and gentlemen, we have a surprise for you all today. This surprise is known to the bride and groom and, with their permission, I would like you all to stand now and turn to face the back please.' He nodded to the organist to begin the wedding march. The bridesmaids came walking slowly up the isle, looking stunning in their in flowing baby pink gowns. The wooden door was then closed while the bridesmaids took their place. There was a slight pause and then the door opened again. Everyone gasped as it opened.

Colleen came walking slowly up the aisle with Charity walking beside her in a beautiful wedding dress! Thomas followed closely behind them, smiling at the guests.

The entire congregation burst out in spontaneous applause.

Michael just gazed in wonder at his beautiful bride. She never took her eyes off him as she walked very slowly and carefully towards him. Thomas walked behind them with a huge smile on his face. He nodded to Richard and Ann, and then to Simone and Paddy - noticing how well they looked together. They walked to the front where the minister motioned to Michael to take his place beside David, who then turned and shook his hand. Thomas placed Colleen's hand in David's, and then Charity's hand in Michael's.

Thomas then took his place beside Mary. ' Today we are handing over both our children to two good people.' He squeezed her hand. She was crying openly now, and whispered in response, 'God is good.'

When the music stopped, the minister spoke again. 'Well my friends as you see this is a very, very special day, as we have the double wedding of David and Colleen, and Michael and Charity. Charity, who has just made it back from Africa a few weeks ago, has been in hiding in order to make this day a big surprise. We must spare a thought for Mr. and Mrs. Sweeney who are losing both their children today - that is, of course, if Michael will say 'I do.' The congregation laughed while Michael nodded, beaming from ear to ear.

Thomas turned to Mary and held her hand, looking fondly into her eyes. 'And here, my love, begins a whole new chapter in our lives.'

Printed in Great Britain
by Amazon